Unraked Hickory Nuts

The Eighth Grade Novel Class of Coach Devon Hind

Simmons Middle School
Hoover, Alabama

Seacoast Publishing
Birmingham, Alabama

Published by Seacoast Publishing, Inc.
1149 Mountain Oaks Drive
Birmingham, Alabama 35226

ISBN 1-878561-89-8

To obtain copies of this book, please write or call:
Seacoast Publishing, Inc.
Post Office Box 26492
Birmingham, Alabama 35260
(205) 979-2909

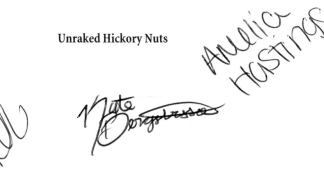

About the Authors

We are a group of eighth grade students from Simmons Middle School in Hoover, Alabama. Each chapter of this book was primarily written by one or two of us, but it was edited and rewritten by the entire class. We assisted each other by giving helpful hints and constructive criticism to "tweak" each chapter. This book is the product of a team effort, and we have therefore decided not to give individual credit for the chapters.

Kate Bergstresser
Philip Binder
Malia Bush
Krys Cooper
Sarah Gillis

Amelia Hastings
Lindsey Higgins
Darothy Mosley
Britany Nichols
Matt Nunnelly

Acknowledgments

We, the eighth grade novel class of Simmons Middle School, 2001, wish to thank many people for helping us with the process of writing this book:

Coach Devon Hind; How can we possibly thank you enough for everything you've done? First of all, for making the class available for us. And, for taking so many hours to help us, especially after school and on the weekends. Thank you for having so much patience with us as we learned. But most of all, thanks for helping us realize how much we can achieve. We have grown as writers and people with your help.

Mrs. Roz Morris; for all her support, taking time out of her busy schedule to come and consult with us, and helping us edit and expand our writing skills.

Mr. Tom Bailey; for being our publisher and encourager. Without him, we wouldn't have been able to get this far.

Mrs. Marilyn Jones (our unit principal); for her expertise about the 70's at Berry High School and support in this project.

Mrs. Carol Barber (our school principal) for giving us her perspective on this topic and support to go ahead.

Dr. Kathy Wheaton (Berry Middle School principal); for allowing our class to freely roam around her school one afternoon and for providing us with pictures.

Mrs. Judy Nysewander; for her cross-country stories of the 70's at Berry High School.

Mr. Mike Wathen; for his cross-country stories of the 70's at Berry High School.

Coach Milton Bresler; for his much needed information on the Berry girls' cross-country teams in the 70's and for letting us use his name as a character.

Coach John Jarmon; for his information on the Mountain Brook girls' cross-country teams in the 70's.

Mrs. Elizabeth Spears; who gave us an inside view of school life at Berry High School in the 1970's.

Mr. Yancy Morris; who gave us information on "working overseas" in the 70's.

Mrs. Russann Wood; who told us how home and work life was back in the 70's.

Mrs. Lynne Roberson; for giving us valuable information about Valley Trailer Park which really did exist in Hoover in the 1970's.

Mrs. Judy Herman; for helping us edit our work.

Mr. Rob Smith, Simmons Middle School band director; for letting some of us participate in the band and this class at the same time.

Coach Kevin Erwin; for letting us "take over" his classroom when we needed extra space and a computer to use.

All of our parents; for taking us on field trips and meeting any other needs we had this year.

Disclaimer

The people and events mentioned in this book are meant to be primarily fictional. Any coincidence of actual characters is unintentional. The only name in our story of an actual person at Berry High School in 1973 & 1974 is Coach Milton Bresler. If you find anything to be offensive in any way, it was unintentional. We hope you enjoy reading our work.

ONE

MY STOMACH WAS DOING FLIPS, partly from anxiety and partly from riding in the car so long. The car smelled of sweet fruit that my mother had packed for the trip. I sat in the front seat of the car, my dog Dusty panting warm, heavy breaths on my neck.

It was a strange day in Hoover, Alabama, 1973. Outside a storm had just passed, and the sky was filled with fog, enveloped in a thick cloud that lasted for miles. Trees with steam swirling around them were visible as far as the eye could see like a misty forest from a fairy tale.

I rolled down the windows as a burst of damp air engulfed my body like a wet towel. We were moving to this new town about 150 miles away from my friends, my school, my house, my life. *I'm really going to miss it, but I'm ready to put the past behind me for Mom's sake.* Since Dad's been gone, Mom has really needed some family support. Our closest relatives lived in Alabama, so there we were.

Thousands of things were running through my mind, and my head ached. *What will school be like? How will the kids act? Will they like me? Will I like*

7

them?

I was roused from my thoughts by a lurch of our old '64 Buick Skylark. There was a symphony of honking cars as we sat in rows of traffic. A small town like Hoover wouldn't normally be this busy, but the interstate had ended in Alabaster, and all the traffic had to go down Highway 31. We turned off the highway into Valley Trailer Park, our future neighborhood, only a half-mile from where the busyness ended at the I-65 entrance ramp.

We had to live in a trailer park then. We moved a lot, so I've lived in as many kinds of houses as one could think of but never in a trailer. I wasn't too thrilled about the idea, but I knew that it could be interesting. I always wondered where all of our money went. *Dad makes a good amount of cash, and here we are living in a portable house and a used one at that. Mom says we're saving up for a permanent home, and we can get one once Dad gets back...if Dad gets back.*

We started up a gradual hill that led to our new home. Rows of trailers, all similar looking, lined the road like books in a row. It was hard to see some of them because of the thickly planted pine trees.

"You know what the best thing about living in Valley Trailer Park will be?" Mom asked.

"Being close to Grandma and Grandpa?" I suggested.

"Well, that will be nice, too, but we'll be within walking distance of Green Valley Drugs where we can get those delicious cheeseburgers and real chocolate milk shakes!" she exclaimed.

"Oh, yeah! Remember how every time we came to visit, I would beg Grandpa to take me there?" My gaze shifted back outside as I spied our new address adorned on a black mailbox. *This must be it.*

"Well, here we are. Home sweet home," Mom said, pulling into the drive.

I stepped out of the car, eager to take my first step into my new home. I surveyed my surroundings hoping that maybe someone my age lived nearby. I left my things in the Buick and swung open the door to the cream-colored trailer. After walking into my new bedroom that my grandparents had already set up for me, I sat on the bed surveying my new quarters. *This is where I'll be living for months to come...my haven from the outside world. A place just my own. My room.*

"Come help me with this luggage, Jade!" my mom yelled. I got my things, went back into my room, piled them on the floor, and sat by the window hoping to catch a glimpse of the neighbors while I started unpacking.

I carefully pulled out my little heart-shaped pot. *Oh, Dad, I miss you so much. Why do things have to be this way? Why couldn't this have happened to anyone but me?!*

I made the pot with Dad in third grade for an art project. The clay was an ugly brown color, and it had a crack down the side, but that didn't matter. It was like a piece of my father...all I had left for the moment.

Just then I heard the storm door rattle. *Someone's*

knocking. My heart started racing. *Who could it be?* Wanting to make a good impression, I quickly glanced in the mirror. I ran to the door, pot in hand. Opening the door revealed a girl who looked to be my age, staring at me with a bright smile. She handed me a foil-wrapped plate. "Hey! I'm Melanie. I live next door. I heard you'd be moving in today, so I made you some cookies," she chimed.

I looked her over. She was sort of tall with shiny, long, blonde hair. Her attitude screamed cheerleader. "Thanks. I can't wait to try one. We only have health food around here," I replied.

"I didn't catch your name..." Melanie said.

"Oh, I'm Jade. Jade Montoya," I stuttered.

"Well, we'll be going to school together. You'll like Berry. You're starting school tomorrow, right?" she asked.

"Right," I answered.

"Do you have any questions about anything?"

"Lots, but I'm used to it. We move a lot," I said, sitting down on the step.

"Really? So do we!" Melanie exclaimed. "My dad's job transfers him all the time, so I know how it feels to be the new kid, too."

"I'm so glad you came over. It'll be nice to see someone I know at school."

"Yeah, so did you move here because of your dad's job?" Melanie asked.

"Sort of, but he's away on the job right now."

"Oh, what does he do?"

"Um, I don't know. Some overseas stuff," I answered.

"That must be tough on you having your dad gone and all." She paused. "Oh, what's that?" she questioned, pointing to the little heart shape sticking out from under the cookies.

"Oh, nothing," I said, embarrassed, as I handed her the warped pot. Suddenly it was all slow motion as the heart slipped from her grasp and fell to the ground. Pieces shattered at my feet.

"Oops," she retorted. "I'm glad it was nothing important." Tears like giant waves swelled in my eyes. I didn't want to cry, but I couldn't help it.

"Gosh, it was just a little pot. I didn't realize it would make you so upset," Melanie said.

"Just a little pot! Oh, you wouldn't understand. No one understands! I...I have to go. Thanks again for the cookies." I slammed the door and ran to my room. Lying face down on the bed, I buried my face in a pillow. I was too upset and tired to sort out my thoughts. I pulled the covers over my head, so Mom wouldn't come in and start asking questions, but it was too late.

"Jade, Sweetie, what happened?" Mom cooed.

"Oh, Mom. I just completely embarrassed myself! Melanie, our new neighbor, broke my little heart pot, and I practically slammed the door in her face! She's going to think I'm a total wacko. I don't know if I'm ready to start school yet. Maybe I should wait another week," I pleaded.

"Jade, don't worry. You have more self-confidence than anyone I know. Just go in there and be yourself."

I figured she was right, but I didn't want to admit it. "Well, okay," I complied.

"You look beat, Honey. Why don't you go to bed early?"

"Mom, I've got too much to do: clothes to pick out, school supplies to organize, and besides, Dusty needs a walk."

"Alright, alright. I'm going to do some unpacking. Yell if you need me."

"Okay," I said.

I fastened Dusty's leash and walked out the door. My heart seemed to break as I saw the shattered pieces that Melanie had pushed into a little pile by the door. I couldn't look at the pot I had once held so dearly, so I quickly jumped off the steps and started running. I didn't know where I was going, but I really didn't care. Hoping the pain in my legs would drown out the pain in my heart, I ran as fast and hard as I could. When I had reached a park called Georgetown Lake, I knew I couldn't run another step. I slowed to a walk, turned around, and tried to remember the way back home. "Dusty," I said, "why did I get myself into this awful mess? I don't think I'll ever be able to explain myself to Melanie. I get a chance to start all over in a new town, and I messed it up already. What do you think I should do, Dusty? I guess I could try to apologize tomorrow. Besides, maybe I can glue the pot back together. Good thing I have you, Dusty. You're always ready to listen. We'll do the best we can, for Mom's sake."

By the time I neared our house, Dusty and I had caught our breath. I gingerly picked up the broken pot and let Dusty follow me into the house. After a hot shower, I sat on my bed trying to somehow put the pot back together, but it seemed hopeless. I set the pieces on the dresser and lay on the bed trying to shift my thoughts to my first day at Berry High School. Before I knew it, I was fast asleep.

TWO

I DID NOT KNOW WHO HE WAS. Looking behind him, he kept running faster and faster. I did not know where he was looking. The glare in his eyes showed fear and anger. Sweat rolled down his muddy face and smeared over his cheeks. The panting of his voice came from deep inside in desperate gasps. The gasps were long-drawn and shaky, like he was struggling to breathe. Who was he?

"Jade. Jade, Honey. Wake up!" I opened my eyes to see Mom hovering over me. "It was only a nightmare."

I sat there for a moment, trying to regain a sense of where I was and glad it was only a dream. "He looked terrified, Mom. He kept running from...from something...grimacing, holding his stomach in pain. I'm not sure what he was running from, but he was really scared."

I've never seen anyone so scared before. Could it have been Dad? I wish I could see him, comfort him. He's always been there when I've needed him. Why can't I be there for him right now? He needs me. We need each other.

"Calm down. It's okay. It's okay..." Mom kept

talking, telling me everything was going to be alright. *She thinks she understands everything, but she doesn't. Nobody understands me. Only my friends, but I had to move. Move away from the life I had loved, the place I was just getting adjusted to. I have to start all over again and meet new friends. Today. Today, I'm going to school. I'm not ready.*

Mom broke the silence, "Go back to sleep. I'll get you up in a few hours."

When I woke up next, it was daylight. I felt like I had been sleeping forever. I pushed all of the blankets off me because I was drowning in sweat. I felt sick. But, I had to go to school because it was the first day. I put on my favorite shirt, a bright blue one with multi-colored flowers encircling the bottom and my favorite slacks, blue and white plaid to match my shirt. I slipped on my buffalo shoes and tied on my shiny silver belt to hold up my pants. I gulped down breakfast and started walking the long mile to Berry High School.

I wanted to ask Melanie about a ride, but I didn't know whether or not she would ever talk to me again. I didn't even know if there was a bus stop around. And, of course, Mom couldn't let me use her car because she had an early job interview that day. *I hope she gets the job so she has something else to do besides worry about me.* My legs were aching as I finally neared Berry. It took forever to walk. I thought I might have gone the wrong way. The school was a bright and disgusting orange color around the windows. I stood in front of a huge mural on the side of

the school. There were five people, each holding
something in their hands to symbolize a certain subject.

I have never been so nervous in my whole life. I
had changed schools before but nothing like this.
Being a junior in high school is bad enough without
having to be the new kid worrying about first impres-
sions. I strained my neck to look at all the thousands
of tiny tiles on the mural, wondering how long it must
have taken to make. It was beautiful. I wanted to
stand there and look at it all day instead of going to
school, but I couldn't. I finally pulled open the door
of the school and stood there looking at all of the
people. And there were certainly a lot more than I
had expected. Some looked sullen, in a hurry, and
others looked happy, gossiping with their friends. I
heard whispers floating around, and laughter filled the
halls.

"Oh, I'm sorry. I didn't see you there." This girl,
who was a little shorter than I with dark brown hair,
almost black, was bending down to pick up the books
she had knocked from my hands. "Hey! I don't think
I've seen you around. Are you new?"

"Yes. I'm looking for Mrs. Dillon's room. Do you
think you could show me where it is?"

While she was telling me she would be glad to
show me around, I was staring at her eyes. She reminded me of a dog. Not her hair or body. She
actually had pretty hair. It was longer than mine and
hung over her shoulders, the dark strands framing her
face. But her eyes were amazing. One was bright

blue like the ocean, and the other was dark, almost black. She had a devious look on her face. Her eyes perched right above her cheeks which were covered with freckles. I followed her down a couple of halls and up some stairs until she stopped in front of a dull-looking door.

"This is Mrs. Dillon's room. Looks like we will have some classes together. So, what's your name?"

"Jade. Jade Montoya. And yours?" I didn't like telling people my name. Only because it was really weird. I was given the name because my eyes were a freaky green...an aqua color...the color of a jade gem-stone.

"My name's Fern," the girl said. We both had crazy names and wild eyes. "Hey, maybe I'll see you at lunch."

Lunch arrived before I knew it. The day had started out great, and I wasn't so nervous after meeting Fern. *I think I could like her.* We talked a while at the lunch table about different things. She was easy to talk to. She would randomly point at people and tell me whether they were troublemakers or cheerleaders, and whether they were smart, dumb, funny or mean. I'm glad she warned me of who was who, the cool teachers, the mean teachers, and who not to talk to. She pointed out so many people. I could only remember a few like this boy named Tripp. He was really tall and skinny. He wore such a large assortment of strange necklaces that it looked as if he would collapse under all that weight. And there was this other guy with sandy brown hair (the color of mine). His name was Clay. He glanced over toward me, gave a quick grin, then sat with the snobs. That's what Fern called them anyway. *But...I think I might actually like him. It must be the smile.*

I noticed that Fern's eyes kept glancing right past me, like she was looking at someone. I turned around to see what she was staring at and saw. As I turned back around, a girl approached the table. Fern said, "And she's stuck-up and fake, always pretending to be something she's not."

It was Melanie. *Melanie...stuck up? What is Fern talking about?* Then I remembered what happened yesterday. *She probably thinks I'm a moron. And rude, too. I slammed the door right in her face.*

"Hi, June. Your name is June, right?" Melanie asked. *At least she thinks she remembers my name. It's close though. I'm just glad she recognizes me.*

"It's Jade."

"Oh, yeah. I'm sorry. How could I forget? About yesterday...I wanted to..."

"It's okay," I interrupted, not wanting to talk about it. "Why don't you sit down?"

"I don't sit here." Before I could ask what she meant, Melanie replied in a cocky voice, "with THEM."

"With who? You mean Fern?" I questioned, wondering what she was saying.

"I mean with the freaks."

For the first time since I met Fern, her expression changed. The steady grin on her face fell, and her blue eye became cloudy. She stood up and left one way while Melanie marched off in the other, having stressed the word, "FREAK." I was left staring at a small, dime-sized teardrop sitting where Fern had been. *She cried. Did I make her do that? No...of course not. Melanie must have. They both left me, and I didn't do anything.*

Snob... Freak... Those words echoed through my mind the rest of the day. *Melanie isn't a snob, and Fern isn't a freak. What did Melanie mean by freak? She looks like a normal person to me, except maybe her clothes and her eyes. But...my eyes are weird, too.*

The day finally ended, and I walked home by myself. I was really upset. *Did I ruin everyone's day?* I didn't know what to do. *Dad would probably tell me to go out and run because that's what he always did. I liked the run yesterday. It helped release most of my frustrations.* Running had made me feel good, like I was doing something worthwhile.

When I arrived home, Dusty greeted me with his usual spunk. "Hey, Boy! Hey there," I said as I stroked his slick fur. "You're such a good dog. Did you miss me? Oh...I bet you did. What did you do all day without me?" I told Dusty all about my horrible day and how lucky he was to be a dog. The biggest problem that he has ever faced is running out of dog food.

After hours of daydreaming and sitting around watching television, I decided to go running again. "Dusty! Come here, Boy. Wanna go for a walk?" At the sound of his name, he cocked his head and ran to the front door, then back to me so I could attach his leash. I finally put the leash on him after he quit jumping around.

We walked outside into the crisp, cool twilight. The stars were fighting free from daylight and beginning to shine between the thick, heavy clouds. Dusty yanked on the leash and I stumbled into a slow jog. We ran a steady pace for what seemed like a million miles.

I would get lost in my thoughts and forget where I was sometimes. I didn't want to think about all the troubles that were going on in my life, but I couldn't help it. My mind kept wandering off to them. *Are Melanie and Fern going to hate each other all year? Forever? Will Dad ever come home? What will he say when he sees the heart pot that Melanie broke?* I didn't like thinking about all of this. *I wish none of it had ever happened. I wish I could start this day all over.*

The sky started getting darker as the sun sank beyond the horizon. The crescent moon had a glowing ring around it and shone proudly in the black sky. The moon was beautiful and reminded me of Clay...bright and dazzling with charm. *He made school one of the few reasons worth going today.* There was not much for me to think about him. All he did was smile. Maybe he didn't mean anything by that smile, but it meant a lot to me...more than he'll ever know. *I can't wait until the day he talks to me. I hope he will soon.*

Lost in thought, concentrating only on Clay and my pace, I realized I had drifted into the middle of the road. I glanced up, dumbfounded, frozen in my tracks. Terror swept over me as blinding bright headlights closed in on me.

THREE

STARS BLINKING WILDLY encircled me as I stumbled out of the ditch. Realizing that a car had almost hit us, I held Dusty close. *Poor dog, he must have been scared to death.* As I stood on the road brushing the dirt off my clothes, a sharp pain shot through my ankle. Grimacing in the dim moonlight, I slowly limped home with my faithful companion. *What is Mom going to say when I get home? If she finds out how careless I've been, she'll never let me walk Dusty at night again... I hope she's already in bed so she won't see me limping.*

As I was nearing our trailer, the living room light switched on abruptly. *Oh, great! Now I WILL have to answer to Mom.* Fortunately, her figure moved to the kitchenette. Moving as quickly as my ankle would allow while trying to ignore the excruciating pain, I quietly opened the door and limped to the shower.

I pushed the covers off the bed and stretched. My eyes opened as the first rays of Alabama sunlight streamed through the windows. I sleepily stumbled to my feet and rummaged through the cardboard boxes

that still cluttered my room. Finally, I found a pair of
shorts and shirt that weren't wrinkled, and then I
dressed. Carrying my books, I walked out the door
and looked back to find Dusty giving me his sad
puppy-face look. "Sorry, Dusty," I told him. "You
have to stay here. I don't want you trying to follow
me to school." He was the best dog. I knew he
would lie patiently on the porch until I came home.

I sat down on the grass at the bus stop next to
Melanie. A couple of minutes later, the yellow bus
stopped with a hiss, and I climbed up to my seat. As
Melanie and I sat together, I hesitantly brought up the
conversation that I had been dreading.

"Melanie. Why wouldn't you sit with me yesterday?"

"What?" She seemed not to remember. "Oh! You
didn't think I would sit with those freaks, did you?"

"Freaks?" I asked.

Melanie continued, "You know...Fern and her little
group of friends."

"What's so bad about them?"

"Let me tell you about freaks, Jade. They're all
weird. Everyday between classes, they go down to the
smoking pit and light up. They're a bunch of rebels.
They don't really care about you. They're just trying to
pull you into their little group. They're not like us,
Jade. They listen to strange music that I'm sure must
have some awful message. They wear bizarre clothes
only because they want the attention."

"Fern didn't seem like that at all!" I exclaimed,
trying to defend my newfound friend.

"Jade, don't hang out with her unless you want to be a druggie."

"She's a druggie?"

"All of those freaks are, Jade."

I felt sick. *What if she is?* I had no time to think because the bus squeaked to a halt, and I was whisked out into the breezeway.

"Hey, Jade," Fern called from around the corner.

"Um...Hey, Fern," my voice quaked with dread.

"Listen...Before class starts, I can take you to meet some of my friends."

She seemed nice enough and didn't sound high or anything, so I decided to follow her. She led me down the concrete walkway through the barren landscape to a stairwell crowded with smokers. Several guys with long hair leaned against the brick wall looking as if they didn't have a care in the world. A few girls stood around, cigarettes in hand with the same nonchalant air about them. "Hey, Guys. This is Jade." I wondered how she could be so bold to address the whole crowd, but they each managed to walk by and introduce themselves. I noticed Tripp from the other day. He seemed pretty nice, so we talked for a while. He wasn't as weird as I would have thought. When he left, Fern told me that he had a pretty rough home-life. Finally, when they all reverted to their previous conversations, I gathered up my courage to address Fern.

"Why do you think Melanie wouldn't sit with us at lunch yesterday? When I asked her about it, she said it was because y'all were freaks, or something, but..."

"Oh, let me tell you about Melanie, Jade. She's not as perfect as you might think. Those jocks and cheerleaders don't care about anybody but themselves. All they want to do is stereotype others to make themselves feel better. They hide behind their expensive clothes and make-up just to be popular. They put up this image of being peppy and smart when in reality they just want everyone's attention. They may not smoke here in the smoking pit where everyone can see them, but they still smoke at the gas stations, where they won't get caught by their coaches and teachers."

"Melanie didn't seem like that," I said. Once again I found myself trying to defend one of my friends.

"You just wait. They aren't what they appear to be. Don't get suckered in just so they can spit you out, Jade. You're too nice." I didn't know what to say. *Are these two groups totally against each other?* I pondered this as I silently slipped away from the growing crowd by the stairwell. *What should I do? It seems like they hate each other, but both of them are such good friends to me.* I sat silently through most of my teachers' lectures while I busied myself by drawing on paper, occasionally taking notes. I was relieved when the bell rang ending my last academic class of the day.

As I walked through the breezeways to the gym, a sharp gust of wind blew through my hair. I saw Melanie and her friend, Dawn, and hoped to casually slip in on their conversation. "Hey, Melanie," I said.

Suddenly without warning, Dawn snapped, "Excuse me! Melanie and I were talking if you didn't notice. Now, would you mind letting us finish our conversation?" She turned around, and acted as if nothing had happened. I felt devastated. *Some people here are so rude.* I looked at Melanie, but when we made eye contact, she quickly glanced away. *That's it. I guess I'll look for Fern and her friends next time. They'll at least pay attention to what I say.*

By the time I made it to gym class, I wasn't feeling too good about myself. Mrs. Davis stuck her head in the locker room and yelled, "Volleyball today, girls."

While all the other girls in the gym sat in their groups and talked, I sat alone in the bleachers and waited for the teacher to enter. Fern eventually shuffled in and took a seat by my side. "Hey, Jade," she said in a dull voice. "What's wrong?"

"Oh, nothing. I'm just becoming more unpopular everyday."

We stopped talking when Mrs. Davis walked in to get our volleyball games started.

"Oh, great! Looks like she'll choose the popular girls to be captains again...the snobs...jocks...whatever you want to call them. We'll probably be the last ones chosen." Fern chuckled halfheartedly.

Finally, Mrs. Davis said, "Alright! Dawn, you and Amanda are captains for volleyball. Go ahead and pick your teams."

"She always chooses the popular people to be captains. Always. Never one of us," commented Fern. *I guess she considers me "one of us" now. Does that make me a freak? Oh, well, what can I lose?*

"You...you're on my team," said Amanda, pointing to the girl standing next to me, a tall swimmer.

"Melanie, you're on my team," said Dawn. *Melanie is my friend...maybe she'll get Dawn to pick me.* But that didn't reassure me. I knew these people wouldn't sacrifice their popularity for a so-called freak like me. *Freak. Freak.* The words rang out in my mind. *Do I consider myself a freak now? Or do I associate myself with them because they are the only ones who will accept me besides Melanie?*

Please don't let me be last. Please!

The choosing continued. After all the probable athletes and cheerleaders were pulled to the teams, all the apparent misfits were left standing with me. *I wonder if they feel the same way as me.* It wasn't fair, how all the popular people were chosen first. Waiting to be picked, I stood in line with Fern.

Finally, after all the unpopular, unathletic, and overweight people had been chosen, Fern and I were the only ones left. Amanda selected Fern while Dawn reluctantly chose me.

"Why don't you stand over there..." She pointed to the back of the gym. "...so you don't mess us up. I don't want to lose because of you," Dawn said in a disgustingly sarcastic voice.

What had I done to deserve that? I wanted to scream, but I held back my anger and tried my best to help the team. Obviously, my best wasn't good enough because Dawn constantly pushed me out of the way to hit the ball. If I did try to hit the ball, Dawn would yell at me for doing it wrong.

Fern spoke up. "Leave her alone, Dawn." She cast Dawn a cold look and then turned to me. "Don't listen to her, Jade. She just wants to show off." *Maybe Fern is the only true friend I have here at Berry for now. At least she's willing to defend me.* At that point I was glad to have her as a friend.

Unable to forget gym class, I found it difficult to concentrate on my schoolwork as I sat through study hall. Finally, the last bell rang, and I boarded the bus.

Not a word was spoken between Melanie and me the whole way home. I guess Melanie got bored with me because she switched seats to talk to another group of people. I didn't care at the time. The bus stopped, and I walked alone to my house. Dusty was right where I had left him. Begrudgingly, I started my homework. I meticulously flipped through the pages of my literature and history books, and when I finally finished my algebra, I closed the book in relief.

Mom made me a small plate of leftover Cajun chicken, and I took it to the living room to join her. The glare of the small television illuminated the tiny room with an eerie blue glow. I stopped, supper in hand, to see what Mom was watching, but when she noticed me, she went over and turned the television off.

"Hey, Honey," Mom said. "Finish your home-work?"

"Yeah, finally. What were you watching?"

"Oh, just some more stuff about that 'Title Nine' legislation."

"Title Nine?" I asked.

"Remember that law passed about a year ago? It allowed girls to do anything boys can do."

"Oh, yeah. You know, I've been hearing rumors that Berry's going to start some more girls' sports soon. Pretty exciting, huh?"

Mom's face drew a perplexed look. *What is she thinking about?* Finally, she snapped out of her deep thought and replied, "I would hope you would never actually BE in those sports, Jade."

"Why wouldn't I, Mom?"

"Because playing sports is intended for boys." Mom's face tensed, and she sounded frustrated. "Why don't you want to be a cheerleader like other girls?"

"Mom, don't you understand? I don't want to be a cheerleader!"

"Listen, Jade. I know what's right for young girls like you."

Inside I boiled with rage knowing where this conversation was heading. "No, you don't, Mom. No, you don't." I left my dinner on the tray and moved toward the door. "I'm going to walk the dog. I'll be back in a little while to finish my dinner." I stepped outside with Dusty's leash. "Come on, Dusty. We're going for a walk."

"Be back before..." I was glad the screen door slammed shut before I could hear what she said.

I walked until I got to the end of our street. Then I started running faster and faster. "Good boy, Dusty." He matched my pace evenly at my side. His rhythmic panting calmed my nerves. We started running up to Georgetown Lake. "Listen, Boy. I don't know what to do about Mom." I must have looked crazy talking to my dog, but I guess that's what happens when you have nowhere else to turn. "She seems obsessed with me being a cheerleader just because she was. I want to do other stuff besides that. We need to think of something to convince her, but what?"

FOUR

"WHOA! YOUR MOM IS WEIRD. I've never met a female so prejudiced against her fellow women," Fern's melodic voice flowed through the receiver.

"Yeah, I know," I responded. "Anyways, you want to go shopping today?"

Without hesitation Fern chirped, "Sure. I'll pick you up in a few minutes. I've got the car for the weekend."

I hung up the phone and changed out of my pajamas and into a pair of worn out jeans and Dad's ratty tie-dyed shirt. The shirt still smelled like him, and a single tear glided down my cheek as my mind flooded with memories. Mom wanted me to dress "as a proper lady should" which entailed frilly dresses, hair bows, and make-up. I would rather just throw something on and go.

I walked down the hall grudgingly, dreading the inevitable contact with Mom. She popped out from the pantry and bounded toward me. I grimaced.

"I'm sooooo sorry about last night, Honey," she gushed. "Me and your grandma are going to lunch today. Why don't you..." She glared at my outfit.

"...put on some decent clothes and join us?"

"Can't," I muttered, trying to portray indifference while boiling inside. The familiar roar of a car engine droned from our driveway. Relieved, I turned away and calling over my shoulder shouted, "I'm going out. I'll be back around mid-afternoon." Mom shrugged her narrow shoulders and sauntered into her bedroom.

Fern and her parents owned a hippie-style VW van. A spray painted mural of peace signs, psychedelic flowers, and scattered Deadhead slogans adorned the rusty exterior. The smoky odor of incense lingered, swirling through the air and infiltrating the upholstery. The distorted speakers churned out the last anthemic verses of Black Sabbath's "Paranoid" as I heaved myself into the passenger seat.

"Like the car?" Fern asked with a sarcastic smile.

"Hey, it could be worse," I told her. "You could have my mom." Fern rolled her eyes, and we laughed. Instantly, I regretted the comment. *Mom isn't that bad, and if Dad were here, my home-life would be perfect.*

We pulled into a Texaco parking lot. "Just gotta get something before we hit the mall," Fern explained as we pushed through the heavy doors into the grimy interior. "Go flirt with the cashier," she ordered, pointing to the tall man of about twenty who sported a flannel shirt, oily hair, and a five-o'clock shadow. I was confused but still proceeded to comply.

The cashier, whose name turned out to be Johnny, was nice and more than willing to play along, but after a moment, I began to wonder what she was up to. Out of the corner of my eye, I spotted Fern scan the room, then pick up a box of something and drop it squarely into her pocket. She hurried back toward me with strong, graceful strides, smiled at Johnny, and stated curtly, "Jade, I changed my mind. Let's go."

Once in the car she pulled the box out of her pocket. It was a pack of Vantage cigarettes. Sensing my shock, she reasoned, "Don't worry, we'll never get caught." Then, almost as if to reassure herself, added, "And if we do... well... we can lie our way out of it. No problem." Fern then tended to the eight-track, replacing Sabbath's crunching guitar riffs with the meandering musical psychedelia of The Doors' debut album. I pulled a stick of incense from a box labeled, "Opium Scented," sniffed it, lit it, and then gingerly slipped it into the wooden burner. Sighing, I slid back into my seat and wondered how Fern could justify a behavior like shoplifting solely on the lack of conse-quences without ever considering the morality.

She could have gotten me into trouble, too. My stomach twisted itself into a knot. *This time we got away with it, but next time we could get caught, maybe even arrested. I should confront her.* But the thought of potentially eradicating my chance of a social life was scary. *If I lose the friends I have now for being a Miss Goody Two-Shoes, I probably won't make any more. Not many others have been very accepting. But I don't want to deny my own principles. I guess I'll do it. I'll confront her.* It was just a matter of how and when.

Fern pulled the van into the parking lot of

Eastwood Mall. We'd been sitting in silence for the past half-hour, and with an air of awkwardness, we jumped out of the van. The sudden shot of Alabama sun mixed with the baking asphalt and created a blinding, steaming atmosphere. *If my hair were wet, it would boil.*

Once inside the revolving door, a buzzing air conditioner provided a welcomed blast of relief, and the dim overhead lighting soothed my eyes. "This way," pointed Fern, and we proceeded to the juniors' racks. Shunning the myriad of brightly colored mini-skirts, she picked a pair of wide, bell-bottomed jeans and handed them to me. I selected a couple of fuzzy, flannel shirts making sure to choose a size too large for me. We found a couple of oversized, plain-colored tee shirts, then topped it off with a comfy, brown leather jacket. Heading toward the front of the store, a lump materialized in my throat as I realized Fern may offer me a cigarette. *I don't want anyone to think I'm a chicken, but I don't want my home to erupt if Mom smells smoke on me, not to mention that I don't want my lungs to turn to charcoal. No,* I reasoned. *She probably only smokes to impress others. She has no need to impress me. I'm the one pressured to prove myself.* Still, I couldn't convince myself.

"We WILL be paying for these," Fern joked in an attempt to revive the light mood.

"I would hope so," I responded forcing an uneasy laugh. Suddenly, noticing a headache, I dug around in my bag and came up with a couple of spherical, white pills. Fern eyed them curiously almost nervously.

"Just aspirin," I assured her, and she visibly relaxed. The bitter coating stuck to my mouth as I swallowed them without water.

Glancing at the checkout line, I reluctantly noted that it would take eons to get through. I considered, then instantly decided against, using the opportunity to confront Fern. I didn't want tempers to erupt in a public setting as might happen in as stressful a territory as a checkout line.

Fern shattered the wall of silence by nailing me with a big question. "So, exactly how thick is the tension between you and your mom?" She seemed genuinely interested, and I detected a hint of hurt in her voice.

I took a deep breath and began. "I'm an only child, and my dad's out on extended business overseas, so it's just us at the house. We have pretty different viewpoints on life, and our personalities clash pretty bad. There's a good deal of bickering, but I guess things aren't too bad."

"Oh, that's not bad at all," she half-whispered, a ghost of vulnerability haunting her normally strong, glaring eyes.

Sensing her need to discuss something, not to mention being overcome with curiosity, I inquired, "What about you?"

Fern sighed deeply, and for a moment I wondered if asking was a mistake. But she began, explaining, "I guess it's obvious my parents are hippies. I'm cool with that. I like The Grateful Dead as much as anybody, and I've fought through a few 'Nam protests myself. But, they're also, well, junkies." She paused, cringing at the word as if it were profane. "They smoke pot constantly, and drink beer like Coke. Normally, my dad's the happiest, most peace-loving guy you'd meet, but sometimes when he's drinking, he..." She choked on her words.

"You don't have to tell me."

"Thanks. I don't think I could say it aloud, anyways." I gasped, shocked. A wave of paranoia splashed me as I noticed the elderly woman to the front of us crane her neck to listen. Fern continued, oblivious to the eavesdropper. "When he's been tripping, it's not that bad, but it'd terrify anyone to see him collapse on the floor, mumbling nonsense. A lot of people expect me to use any chemical that comes my way, what with me being the supposed 'bad girl,' and all. But, I've vowed not to touch anything but cigarettes." She appeared relieved to have thrown such a lofty weight off her shoulders.

"Gosh. I...uh...I'm so sorry," I stammered, too shocked to know what to say. Luckily, we had reached the end of the line. The conversation reached a natural end as I paid for my clothes.

The sun once again stunned and paralyzed my eyes as we left the store. "Pretty darn hot out here, huh?" Fern asked.

"Yep," I agreed. "Alabama is one big incinerator compared to the weather in some of the places I've lived."

The heat of the metal door handle seared my hand turning it red for a moment, and the vinyl seat burned my legs through my jeans. As Fern climbed in, I felt a pang of sympathy for her as I rethought the confrontation I had planned about the shoplifting. Before today she seemed like a stone wall, never flinching in the face of adversity. After the conversation in the line, the thick skin peeled away to expose a tender heart. I did not want her to feel as though everyone was on her back.

Gripping the wheel, she assumed a manner of mock seriousness and declared, "Well, you're a freak now. Congratulations." I laughed, she cranked the ignition, and the aged exhaust pipe spit a cloud of black smoke.

Will I still be laughing after I confront her, if I ever do? I wondered silently. *Sure hope so.*

Fern reached into her pocket and retrieved the dreaded pack of cigarettes. My stomach flipped as she held one out for me and asked in an untaintedly casual voice, "Want a smoke?"

FIVE

A WAVE OF ANGER flushed all pity for Fern out of my system. *Doesn't she know I'm not like that?* I drew a deep breath, and then all my thoughts began gushing through my mouth. "What is wrong with you?" I shouted. "Shoplifting is illegal. And on top of that, it's morally wrong. Did you ever consider that? Or do you only think about what you can get away with?"

"And this smoking. You've seen firsthand what drugs can do to a person. Nicotine IS a drug. It's more dangerous than pot, and it'll screw you up just as bad as all the garbage your parents are using. You're acting totally reckless doing this stuff. You only see what you want to see, and worse, you're being an absolute hypocrite!"

Relieved, I sighed. Fern's thoughts were masked by a completely blank look. I hoped she might combust like I had, but she coldly refused to allow me the satisfaction. "Oh, I'm sorry," she stated, voicing each syllable strongly, yet calmly. "I didn't know it was your job to analyze my life. I'll try to remember that next time." She cleverly avoided all eye contact when she talked. We sighed in unison, turned up the radio, and rode home, suffocated by a heavy silence.

When I stormed into the tiny trailer, Mom asked, "Did you have good time?" I threw her a look that meant, "I don't want to talk about it." For once, she understood. I marched off to my room and tossed the bag of clothes on the floor.

"Jade, are you hungry? I've got supper ready," Mom yelled.

"Yes, Ma'am. Let me change into my new clothes so I can show you," I replied.

I opened the bag and pulled out the pair of blue jeans and tee shirt. *These are so comfy. No wonder Fern likes them.* I put on the new outfit and strutted into the kitchen. Mom looked totally horrified. Her eyes widened to look like golf balls, her mouth hung half-open, and she was speechless for a few seconds. After that, anger overcame the initial shock.

"What is THAT? Don't tell me you used MY hard-earned money on THOSE clothes," Mom snipped.

"I didn't WASTE your money. This is what all my friends wear," I retorted.

"Jade, what am I going to do with you? I was never this much trouble for your grandmother. Sit down and eat," Mom sighed.

"I'm not hungry anymore," I huffed as I returned to my room. *What's wrong with her? Ugh, I thought she understood! Why can't she let me be me! And besides, when did she become a fashion genius? She'd probably pick out a frilly Sunday-picnic dress.* I turned on the clock radio beside my bed. Led Zepplin's

"Stairway to Heaven" came blasting through the speakers. *That's way too loud.* I quickly turned it down before Mom became further aggravated, and I flopped down on the bed. *I'm too tired to move.* My thoughts drifted back to Fern as the music faded into the back of my mind. *I'll bet Fern's parents would think these clothes are cool. Yeah, they'd understand completely.*

The sunlight streaming through my window caused my sleepy eyes to open. Dusty was lying at the end of my bed. "Hey, Boy. How'd you get in here?" I murmured as I patted his silky, golden fur. I yawned and rolled over. *Mom must have come to check on me...that's how Dusty got in. I must've fallen asleep before I changed. I glanced down at my jeans. I can't wear these to church; Mom would have a fit. Do I have time to take a shower?* I glanced at the alarm clock. I had plenty of time. I grabbed a towel, and headed to the bathroom.

I woke up late again Monday morning and nearly missed the bus. I ran up to the stop as the bus was turning the corner. Melanie stood there looking like her usually preppy, perky self.

"Mornin' Jade!" she piped. "I waited as long as I could at the tree, but..."

"I know. Sorry," I mumbled. *How can she look so perfect and perky so early in the morning? Not only did I just roll out of bed, but I probably look like it too.* The bus jerked to a stop, and we climbed on and slumped into a brown bench seat.

"So, how do you like my new clothes?" I asked Melanie.

"Well...umm...they're really...uh...you could say..." Melanie stuttered.

"Never mind," I said. *I don't want to know.* The bus pulled slowly up to the school just a few minutes before the bell rang. I navigated my way through the halls to my locker. I dreaded going into Mr.Grant's room where Fern would be in her assigned seat next to mine. *I really hope she's not mad at me.* I took a deep breath and slunk into the room.

"Hey Fern," I paused. "Umm... about Saturday... I didn't mean...." I stopped as she turned her hard, bitter eyes toward me. She glared at me a moment before speaking.

"Jade, it really hurt me that you would criticize me so badly..." Her eyes turned soft and loving. " ...but you cared enough to tell me." Fern rose. We stood there awkwardly a few seconds before hugging. "Thanks," she whispered, trying hard not to cry. *Wow!* I couldn't think of any possible way to respond. Fern looked so vulnerable like when she had told me about her mom and dad.

I struggled to find words, and finally I said, "Anytime. Besides...what are friends for? But...I shouldn't have been so hard on you." I spent the rest of class trying to do my work while thinking about how great it was to have such a good friend.

* * *

Several months later...

After first period, I found Melanie in the hall.

"Hey, Jade. Do you think you can be on time tomorrow morning? It seems as if you're late half the time," Melanie teased.

"Yeah, it's just tough getting up so early on Mondays," I explained.

I felt someone hovering over my shoulder. "That's nothing. The guys on cross-country have morning workouts at six," Dawn remarked coldly, as she butted into our conversation.

"Oh! Cross-country!" Melanie exclaimed, trying to stop Dawn from saying anything further. "Did you hear? They're gonna have a girls' team next year. It sounds like fun."

A girls' cross-country team? That DOES sound like fun! Dad always told me about how much he loved to run in high school. That would be so cool! Doesn't that guy Clay run cross-country?

"Can anyone join?" I asked.

"What?" Melanie said, her nose scrunched up and her eyebrow slanted downwards. I had never seen such a strange look on her face.

I paused before remarking uneasily, "I meant...can I join?" They both looked at me like I was an alien or some sort of two-headed monster. "It sounds neat. I was wondering if I could be on the team or maybe who to talk to about it."

Out of nowhere, Dawn burst into fits of laughter. "You know... for a freak... that's a pretty good joke!" Dawn roared.

"You are joking, aren't you, Jade?" Melanie questioned.

"Uh...yeah...of course," I lied, trying to keep the disappointment out of my voice. The two of them still giggling sauntered away. I stood there, watching them curiously until they blended into the crowds of people. *What's so funny? I'll ask Fern.*

Finally... the last class of the day, study hall. I'll have a chance to ask Fern about cross-country. I plopped down in the seat next to Fern and set my books on the floor. I still couldn't get over how Melanie and Dawn laughed so hard. *Why would they laugh at me? Do they think I can't run? Or do they just not like me? I thought Melanie was my friend.*

"Jade, you okay?" Fern inquired. "You haven't said a word since you sat down."

"Well...in the hall after first period, I was talking to Melanie when Dawn came up. Melanie said there was gonna be a girls' cross-country team next year. I thought it sounded like fun, so I..."

Fern cut me off. "Whoa...cross-country? Fun? You're joking, right? Jade, you know WE don't do sports..."

"Of course. I was kidding! Man, I sure got y'all good!" I replied as Fern laughed and I faked it. *No, I'm not joking! Why does everybody think this is a big joke? Maybe I shouldn't run. But I love to run! It's this whole jock, freak thing again. Ughhhhh!*

By the time I got home, I had been thinking non-stop about cross-country. When the screen door squeaked open, Dusty, who was lying in the kitchen, jumped up and bounded toward me.

"Have you been lying here all day? Did we forget to put you out this morning? Here, I'll let you out now, and I'll take you for a walk later."

Dusty's ears edged forward and his tail wagged eagerly at the word "walk". After letting Dusty out, I headed into my room and flounced down on the bed. I had a ton of English and science homework since I really hadn't been paying attention in class. Eager to go "walking" with Dusty, I rushed through it. Finally at four-thirty I finished. I slipped into some running shorts, a tee shirt, and some old sneakers. *Where's Dusty's leash? Maybe Mom put it by the door.* I scoured the trailer in a frantic search for the leash. *Where on Earth could it be?* Mom, tired from work, came through the door.

"Hey, Jade. Have a nice day?" she inquired. "Are you taking Dusty for a walk?"

"Uh, yes Ma'am," I responded, "How'd you know?"

"He's sitting outside with the leash in his mouth," Mom said as she set her bag down on the couch. I treaded outside and sure enough, Dusty was sitting there with the leash. I tried to look mad but cracked up laughing.

"Come on, Boy, let's go," I said as I retrieved the leash from his mouth and clicked it on his collar.

The sun had started to set in a whorl of fuschia reds and golden yellows. The trees barely cast shadows along the road. Dusty and I walked briskly until I was sure Mom couldn't see us anymore. I started a fast jog. A few minutes later, my breath came in short pants, and my legs pounded heavily on the ground. *What's so wrong with loving this? This is when I feel best. Why doesn't anyone think running is right for me? Melanie and Fern...I thought they were my friends. They're supposed to support me. Dad would want me to run. Actually, Dad wouldn't care what I did, as long as I loved what I was doing. Yeah, if Dad were here, he'd be behind me 100%. What would Mom say if I told her I wanted to do cross-country? She still probably wants me to be a cheerleader...just like her. I don't wanna be Mom all over again. Besides, according to Fern I can't do ANY sports. That's stupid. I don't want to be labeled a freak. I don't want to be labeled a jock either. What's wrong with me just being Jade Montoya? Not a freak. Not a jock. Just Jade.* I slowed down to a walk, so by the time we were back, we would have time to catch our breath. I passed by Melanie's trailer. One window was open, and I could see her family sitting down for supper. Melanie's mouth moved hurriedly, looking really excited. *Probably telling them how psyched she is about cross-country.* I stopped at my front stoop and sat down.

"What do you think?" I asked Dusty. "Run like I want to or be a freak like I'm perceived to be?"

Naturally and logically, Dusty didn't answer, but he was helpful just the same. I knew he had no clue what I was talking about, but something in those round, soulful eyes gave me the impression that he understood. No matter how old he was, Dusty still had sweet, puppy eyes. He laid his silky head loyally in my lap.

"Hmmm...I figured you didn't have much to say. You're a good listener, though. This is really stressing me out. If I run, I'll be considered a jock and risk losing Fern. But, if I don't run, then I won't be happy, and I'll be considered a freak. I don't want to be a freak OR a jock. I just wanna be Jade. What should I do, Dusty?" I looked once more at him and sighed.

*What would Dad say? There must be something...*I racked my brain for memories of Dad and every word of his guidance he'd ever offered me. "What was it that Dad said at the airport before he left? It was so cold that day." I paused, thinking hard. "Oh, how could I forget!" *Jade, you're my special little girl. I love you. Don't ever forget that. Everyday, you make me prouder and prouder. You care about others. Remember that time you found a baby bird that had fallen out of its nest in the backyard? You stayed and nursed that little bird back to health. And that little boy... what was his name? Well, nobody liked him and he didn't have any friends. Then, you went over and played with him everyday. You can look past people's flaws and see their strengths. Don't lose that.* I wiped a tear from my eye as Dusty looked up at me. "I miss him so much, Boy. Don't you?" *You're independent, too, Jade. In kindergarten, the teacher gave everyone a picture of an apple tree to color. All the other kids colored their apples red, but you liked them purple. And even when you saw that yours was different from everybody else's, you kept coloring them purple. You certainly have always been your own person. Don't let anyone change who* *you are. I'm gonna be praying for you and your mother everyday. Anyway, I'll be back before you know it. Don't forget to play with Dusty for me.* I smiled through my tears as I patted Dusty's silky head. "Thanks, Dad. I know exactly what to do now."

SIX

I WOKE UP SHAKING as visions from my nightmare flashed through my head. I tried to calm myself as the once vivid scenes turned to mere memories. My cheeks were wet with tears, and a salty spot had formed on my pillow. Struggling to block out the thoughts left over from my dream, I dressed slowly. I walked down the hall trying to collect myself as my rumbling stomach signaled that it was breakfast time. I was glad to see Mom facing the other way as she prepared my ritual oatmeal breakfast. She turned around to set out my glass of milk and gave me a heartbroken look as she saw my tear-stained eyes.

"What is it, Jade? Another nightmare?" she asked as she pulled me into her arms. I let all of my feelings release as I sobbed into Mom's silky white pajamas.

"Oh, it's just so awful," I cried. "Dad is so far away, and I need him here. I just don't know if I can go on without him, Mom. I just don't know anymore."

"Oh, Honey...I feel the same way. We both miss Dad, but we have to be brave for him. Soon, his time will be up, and he'll be home before we know it."

As we shared the remainder of our tears, I realized

that for one of the first times my mom and I were really bonding. It felt good that for once we were both on the same side. I knew that it was one of those defining moments in life—one of those things that you can't help but remember forever.

I couldn't eat my oatmeal because my throat was still tight with emotion. Mom glanced at the clock and said that I had better head out before I was late for school. I gathered my things together and stood at the door staring at a family portrait. Dad's hair was perfectly combed, every strand in place. I laughed between sobs as I remembered how meticulous Dad was about his hair. He wore a stern grin, and pride showed through his venturing eyes. His smile seemed to tell me everything was going to be okay.

Staring at the door, I mustered up all my courage and held back the tears so Melanie wouldn't see me crying. I took a deep breath and bounded out the door.

"Have a good day. Everything will be okay," Mom hollered.

Outside, I saw the thin silhouette of Melanie leaning against a tree waiting for me. Hearing my footsteps, she turned toward me, and we started walking to the bus stop.

"Jade, are you okay? What's the matter?"

I knew that if I had to explain to her I would be sobbing in a minute.

"You wouldn't understand," I managed.

"How do you know I wouldn't understand?" She started walking faster. "You never tell me anything, so how can I?"

Flipping her hair, she stomped off ahead of me. I watched her footsteps get further and further away. An empty feeling came over me as I realized that I might have suddenly lost a friend. *I can't go to school now—not with her being mad at me. She's probably thinking awful things about me. I didn't mean to upset her. Great! Another horrible day and it has hardly even started.* I kept walking, my shoelaces untying more with each step.

When I arrived at the bottom of the hill three trailers away from the bus stop, I decided I was tired of school. I didn't want to see Melanie. Or Fern. Or anybody. *Practically everyone I do see doesn't LIKE me, doesn't KNOW me, or is MAD at me. The whole world's mad at me—my world anyway.*

I turned around and started back up the hill, dragging my feet along, stirring up dirt, and kicking pebbles. *I don't feel like going to school today. Or ever again.* My shoelaces were getting dirty and really annoying me. I looked back for Melanie, but she was already gone.

I finally bent down to tie my shoelaces and re-membered how Dad taught me to tie them when I was a little girl—*loop, swoop, and pull the bunny ears. I wish he could be here to teach me something more important like how to tie my life together.* I sat down on the side of the street because I had nowhere else to go but home. I sat there thinking about Dad and started crying again. My teardrops got bigger, and I felt one trickle down my cheek. I watched it fall to the ground.

I looked at it, wondering why I was crying. The tears spread out at first, melting into the hard clay, but soon began to form a tiny puddle. I started to get up from the ground when I noticed a tiny ant crawling toward my growing pool of tears. I watched it get closer until it seemed like the puddle sucked it in. As the ant struggled to save itself, I started feeling sorry for it. I don't know why, but I reached over and killed it. Guilt poured over me. *I took the life of that poor, defenseless, little creature.* It's the first time it ever bothered me to kill a little ant. I guess I did it out of habit.

People take life for granted, even me. We see violence and death around us so much that it seems as if we've become calloused to the value of life. A lot of people don't really pay much attention to all the killing going on in our world, including me. I see people everyday on television blowing others up...shooting them...or tricking each other into death. The news is filled with the death tolls from Vietnam. Are they killing people because they consider it their job? Has it become habit to them? Do they feel like murderers when they take those lives like I do right now? Or do the soldiers ever even think twice about it? Some people find news of Vietnam the most interesting thing on television, and war looks like a game to them. I was starting to realize how serious war really is. *Life is not something to take for granted, Jade. When people least expect it, death can enter their world and the preciousness of time becomes clear. I'm just as bad as anyone. I'm contrib-*

uting to death in this world. What did that ant ever do to me? I begrudgingly picked myself up from the ground and headed home.

All day long I thought about death. I figured that dealing with death was the hardest part of life. I spent the day on the couch with Dusty watching *All My Children* and some other soap operas and then finally *Leave It To Beaver.* I started getting frustrated because they were too predictable, and I knew everything that was going to happen: Beaver and Wally get into a fight and make up at the very end just in time to finish the episode. *Life isn't REALLY like that. Problems come along, and you can't just fix them in a second. Words are irreversible, just like death. Once you say them, there is no taking them back. Words can scar a friendship and hurt the heart even after problems have mended.*

Noticing the mail had come, I went out to see if there was anything for me. As I walked back inside, I hurriedly flipped through the mail and stopped short, seeing Dad's handwriting addressed to me. I ripped open the envelope and started reading.

Dear Jade,

I'm sorry I haven't been able to write sooner. I've been really busy over here. How are you two doing? I'm doing fine, so don't worry about me. I miss you two so much! I'm counting down the minutes until I can see you and Mom...

After finishing the letter, I sat back down on the couch as Dusty climbed up and laid his head on my knee. I felt really dumb about lounging around having a pity party all day. *You've made things worse now, Jade. Mom's going to find out and get mad.* "Skipping school won't change anything...will it, Dusty? I'll have to go back eventually. I'm going to stop running from my troubles and face my problems head on." I stroked Dusty's golden hair as he looked at me with his big brown eyes. "I have to be willing to work through my difficulties. There are bigger things to cry about. If Dad can survive his hardships, then I have nothing to worry about...except him."

SEVEN

I WALKED INTO THE CLASSROOM wondering what lay ahead of me for the rest of the day. Hoping nobody would ask where I was yesterday, I took my seat in the middle row of Miss O'Neal's class. "Good morning," Miss O'Neal said when she walked into the room and shut the door. Her constant optimistic attitude was one of the first things that made me feel welcome to this new school. "Hey, Jade. We missed you yesterday. Were you sick?"

"Sort of," I responded. I knew I had just lied, but the whole class was listening. If I had given the real reason, they wouldn't have understood.

"I'm sorry to hear that," she said in a sympathetic tone. "Do you have an excuse?" I pulled a torn piece of paper out of my pocket, walked up to her desk, and placed it in her hand. *Mom is very understanding. She didn't even raise her voice when I told her the reason for staying home yesterday.* Miss O'Neal quickly read my note and brushed it aside. In a quiet tone, she continued, "Oh, Jade...I've been meaning to mention something to you." I felt nervous as I waited to hear what she had to say. "I'm going to be helping

Coach Bresler out next year with the girls' cross-country team. Are you interested?"

I paused for a moment and let the news sink in. *Wow, Miss O'Neal wants ME on her team. But, what will Mom say? What will Fern say? She won't agree with it at all. She'll try to tell me about how bad all jocks are. And Melanie...what will she think?*

"Jade?" Her voice brought me back to reality.

"Umm...I'm not really sure," I said.

"Oh, come on, Jade. I really want you to do it," she said with a serious smile that told me she really meant it. "I've seen you at night, running with your dog. You'll do fine."

"Oh...alright. I guess it would be fun," I answered.

"Great! We sure can use as much talent as we can get." She paused, then walked to the front of the room, leaving me by her desk. "Oh, class, I've been meaning to tell you. As you all know, because of the passing of "Title Nine" legislation, there will be additional girls' sports here at Berry. I'm going to be the assistant coach of the girls' cross-country team. If any of you are interested please let me know. Jade's going to do it...aren't you, Jade?" She looked at me and flashed another smile. I could feel my whole face starting to get hot as the entire class looked at me. A few of them snickered. I knew that someone was going to say it. Any moment now, somebody was going to say something rude about me running.

"Freaks don't run!" somebody whispered so that I could hear. Miss O'Neal obviously didn't hear the comment. Feeling terribly embarrassed, I made my way back to my seat and tried not to make eye contact with anyone in the room. *I don't care what they think. I'll run if I want to. I'm not going to let them discourage me.* The bell finally rang dismissing me from what seemed to be one of the longest homeroom times I have ever had. I quickly gathered my books and hurried to tell Fern what I was planning to do.

Trying to make a way to my locker, I pushed my way through the crowded halls of Berry High School. As I approached it, I saw Fern eagerly waiting for me.

"Hey, Fern!"

"Why are you so happy? Oh, don't tell me you've been hanging around those cheerleaders again," she joked.

"Ha, ha." I forced a sarcastic laugh. "No. I've decided to run cross-country next year. I guess some girls want to form a team in the fall. I guess that they couldn't say 'No' because of that 'Title Nine' thing. Isn't that great? Miss O'Neal asked me to be on the team. Do you think you'd like to run, too?" I paused, surprised by the expression on Fern's face. She was looking at me like I was some kind of idiot.

"The other day I thought you said that you were joking! Why in the world would I want to do something like that? Of course, I'm not running next year. We don't DO sports. We aren't THAT kind of people, Jade. I thought you knew that," she said as her voice grew louder. *Wow, she gets mad easily. I'm tired of this jock and freak thing. I don't care if I'm considered a freak or not. I'm going for it. Fern can't stop me, and nobody else can, either!*

"Well..." I looked for an answer to give, "...I enjoy ru-"

Fern cut me off. "Jade, they'll never accept you. Wait and see...you'll never fit in. They consider you like one of us now, a freak. I can't believe Miss O'Neal actually planted such a crazy idea in your head. She must be new at this. Everybody knows that freaks don't run. They think that we're just a bunch of lazy bums that sit around and smoke pot all day. They don't believe in us. They don't think that we're capable of doing anything as good as them. Those stupid jocks!"

Some people were starting to look at us now. I knew Fern didn't care who listened. She was going to get her point across regardless. The tardy bell was about to ring, so everyone hurried to class. "We'll talk about this some more at the smoking pit after sixth," Fern said as she walked off.

Fern has some strong opinions about the jocks that I don't think I'll ever completely understand. I quickly gathered my books for class and hurried off, so I wouldn't get into trouble for being late. I turned the corner in a rush and sprang up the stairs taking two at a time to math class. I jerked to a stop, almost running into Mrs. Dillon, as my math book came tumbling out of my arms. *Gosh, I really need to find something to carry all of these books in. It's a real pain dropping them all of the time.* I looked up and saw that all-too-familiar look on her face.

"Slow down, right now, young lady," she said in

her usual raspy voice. She shook her finger in front of my face as if I didn't know whom she was talking to. "Now, I've told you before. Young ladies are NOT to be running and jumping around here. This is a school, not a circus!" I had heard this same speech too many times before.

I knew better than to run up that set of stairs. Mrs. Dillon was always standing there. It was instinct, I guess. "Umm...Yes, Ma'am," I said slowly. *Everyone tells me, "Young ladies don't do this, young ladies don't do that." Why can't they leave me alone? Mom is constantly on my case about that. Wait until she hears that I'm running cross-country next year! What will she say then? I'm REALLY dreading that conversation.*

After sixth period I met Fern and the rest of our friends at the smoking pit. Fern had already told the group about my plans. "So, I hear you're turning jock now," someone quipped.

I immediately turned to face Travis, looking him straight in the eye and boldly blurted, "Well, I've decided to run next year if that's what you mean." He flung his head back to get the shoulder-length black hair out of his eyes, and a few others shot out absurd comments and questions. I responded to each one of them just as quickly. Fern never did come to my aid. She stood back, arms crossed, nodding, as if to say, "I told you so."

When the dismissal bell finally rang, I found myself dreading home. *What will Mom say?* My mind was full of questions about cross-country, so I went by Miss O'Neal's room to get some more information about it. As I approached the room, I heard two adults talking. I turned the corner and took a few steps into the classroom.

"Hey, Jade," she greeted me. "I was just telling Coach Bresler about you. This is Jade Montoya, the one from my homeroom."

"Great! Glad you're going to run!" he said as he was leaving.

"Jade, can I help you with anything?" she asked.

"Uh...Yes, Ma'am. I was wondering if you could tell me more about summer workouts and practices and stuff."

"Okay...well...I have a meeting I'm already late for. Here's an information sheet if you want to look over it tonight. I'll talk to you about it more tomorrow in homeroom." She picked up a few papers she had lying on her desk and hurried out the door. I looked up at the clock and realized that I was about to miss the bus. I ran down the stairs, then slowed for a moment, as I remembered what had occurred there earlier in the day. *'Young ladies are NOT to run and jump'.* I sprang out the front door hoping I hadn't missed the bus. A pit in my stomach swelled as I saw the last bus turning onto Columbiana Road. *Great! I'll be walking home all by myself!* I started the long mile back to the trailer park. I was lost deep in thought wondering how to tell Mom that I was going to run on the team when I heard a car engine approaching from behind. I turned around, just in time to see two boys hanging out the windows of a '68 GTO. "Freaks don't run!" one of them shouted. Their laughter poured out of the car as it roared off. *Those idiots.*

I was finishing a chocolate milk shake from Green Valley Drugs when I found Dusty waiting to greet me at his usual spot on the front porch. We went inside and spread out on the couch. Mom was not home yet. *How am I going to tell her? She's not going to like the idea. I know she won't.* I started on my homework to take my mind off of everything. Before I knew it, Mom came strolling through the door.

"Jade...Can you help me with the groceries please?"

"Yes, Ma'am." I dragged myself out of my comfortable seat and went to help her. I gently picked up a grocery sack and smelled the sweet aroma of fruit. We always had fresh fruit somewhere in the house because Mom loved it.

"So...How was your day?" she questioned.

"Oh...It was fine." I wanted to tell her right then, but my mouth wouldn't form the words. As I was putting the soup on the shelf, I couldn't contain myself any longer. "I'm joining the cross-country team next year," I blurted. *There...I did it!* She looked up from the bag of groceries and gave me a startled look.

"No, you're not!" Mom declared. "Why would you want to do such a stupid thing?"

"Stupid? Running's not stupid!"

"Well, it is for girls! I already told you...I don't agree with girls doing those kinds of sports. If you want to do a sport, do cheerleading."

"Cheerleading's not a sport! Mom...please...I really want to do this." I tried giving her one of my most sympathetic looks. "Please..." I pleaded.

"Jade, you know how I feel about this. If you do it, I'm not going to be very happy about it," she said.

"Fine," I said, ending our argument. I stormed off to my room and lay on my bed staring at the ceiling until Dusty pushed the door open and jumped onto my stomach. He perked his ears up and had a puzzled expression on his face.

"Hey there, Buddy. You'll support me, won't you, Boy? Yes...You'll always be there for me! Know what? Mom did say, 'If...' That's a good thing. You know...I can't worry about what other people think I should do! I can't let them discourage me. I won't!" Dusty nudged my arm, trying to lift it up as if he was trying to tell me that he agreed.

EIGHT

MR. GRANT LECTURED about the present perfect tense of verbs from the front of the classroom, as if seniors in high school really care about those sorts of things. "Now, when you want to change a verb from the future perfect tense to the present perfect tense, you..."

"Psssssst! Jade! Jade!" Clay whispered from behind me. I had made sure I "accidentally" sat in front of him.

"What?" I said as I turned around.

"Melanie said you're coming out for cross-country. Are you?" he asked.

"Yeah, I am. I've been waiting all summer for it to start."

"Cool! You'll like it a lot. We do lots of groovy stuff. Free days are the best because you get to go wherever you like. Oh, and the Sears Loop is hard but fun. Everybody stops off at Sears to get water. Coach never finds out though. I think it's really great that they're letting the team be co-ed now." Clay had the biggest grin on his face. *How on earth could God make a guy this cute? There's only one problem...he cusses sometimes. But since he's so good-looking, who cares! I can look past that.* While I was spaced out, thinking about Clay, he was still rambling on about cross-country. "... lots of hard practices, but it makes you better. We play tag or run on the trails the days before races so we don't get too tired for the meet the next day. Everybody hangs out in Coach Bresler's room after practice."

"Sounds great! I'm really excited," I said with a grin.

"Excuse me, Miss Montoya, Mr. Thompson. Is there something you would like to share with the rest of the class?" Mr. Grant then paused for a second. "Well? Okay then...I guess not. Now, Mr. Thompson, would you be so kind as to tell me the present perfect tense of walk?"

"Ummmm, well, you..." Clay stuttered. "Briiiiing." The bell for the end of class rang, and everyone stood up to leave.

"Saved by the bell," Clay said to me as we hurried out of the classroom.

"After being the state champs last year and four out of the last six years, I have high hopes for this team. I think the boys can win it all again. Girls, you can shoot for being the first-ever women's state champs. That would be an amazing legacy to leave behind." Coach Bresler paused to look at our facial expressions. "I'm looking for leaders. A leader has to be courageous, sacrificing, and willing to take risks. I expect cross-country to be one of your top priorities, not something you come out and do whenever you feel like it. Also, I expect you to work as hard as you can, but don't be stupid. If I tell you to have an easy run, run easy. Any one of you pulling a muscle trying to be a big shot is not what I want. Don't give me less than your best. If we're going to repeat as state champs, there's going to be pain to endure. You only get as much out of anything as you put into it. There will come a time when you'll feel like you can't go on, but DON'T...EVER...QUIT! If you're too tired to run, walk. If you're too tired to walk, crawl. But quit? NEVER! Now, let's begin our first workout! Everyone's going to Star Lake today. Boys, I'll meet you there for an interval workout. Girls, you'll be running to the lake too. Since this is your first practice, you can rest for a few minutes when you get there and then head back. When you get back to school, you're through. By the way, since it's so hot today, if you know of anyone who lives near the lake and is willing to share his garden hose, you can get a drink. But, get permission first."

"I live right by the lake! It's fine if everybody gets a drink from my hose!" Tom volunteered.

It was difficult to pay attention to the coach because my eyes kept wandering to where Clay was sitting with his group of friends. Short, sandy blonde hair fell in waves around his head and piercing blue eyes stood out because of his long, golden lashes. Just by looking at him, I could tell he was in shape. *Who's that girl next to him? Oh, Dawn.* I snapped out of my little daydream as Coach Bresler added, "All right, now. Don't forget everything I just told you. I'll see y'all at Star Lake." We left Berry and started down Columbiana Road. Clay ran with Coach Bresler and the top runners from last year's team. The first quarter-mile, I tried to keep up with them, but soon realized that if I kept up their pace, I would be dead by the half-mile mark. Even though I wasn't at the very front, I felt good with my position. A few of the slower guys were back with me, and I had even passed two of them. A few girls ran about fifty yards ahead of me, so I was toward the middle of the pack. My legs were already starting to ache when we passed Hancock Fabrics, but that just made me push harder. *I love every minute of this.*

As we turned left off of Deo Dara and onto Spruce Drive, Dawn whined, "Oh, my gosh! I'm getting all sticky and nasty! And my hair is falling down!" *Of all the people to run next to. Why did it have to be her?*

"Uh, that's what happens, Dawn." I replied matter-of-factly.

"Jade, you don't know anything about cross-country," she panted. "My dad was the top cross-country runner on his team. My mother said that I should run cross-country to stay in shape for cheerleading tryouts. Why are you out here? None of your freak friends are gonna come out and cheer for you at meets. They know better than to TRY and be a jock."

I'm not going to stoop to her level and reply to that. I sped up ahead of Dawn so she couldn't annoy me anymore. The sun pounded down on my back and made little beads of sweat roll down my face, arms, and legs. The asphalt road reflected the blazing heat waves back at me. Although I had been training all summer with Dusty, the heat seemed ten times worse since it was mid-afternoon and not late at night. *Hoover's hot! How am I ever gonna run in this heat every day?* After what seemed an eternity, I reached Star Lake. The sunrays that had tortured me for so long now made the water glimmer brilliantly.

Clay sat at the picnic table cutting up with his friends. Melanie came up about a minute after me and didn't look too good. Her hair was frizzed out in the front and looked damp from sweat. Her shirt was soaked and clung to her. Melanie's legs looked funny from all the red splotches. *I wonder if I look like that, too. If I do, I hope Clay doesn't notice.* In spite of her appearance, Melanie was still grinning and peppy.

"Hey, Jade. So I guess you're really one of us now!" she blurted with enthusiasm.

"One of who...what?" *I'm totally confused.*

"A jock, Jade! You're awesome at running. I mean, you should definitely be in our top five scorers. And you definitely have the look of a cross-country runner!" she said, grinning madly.

"Are you saying I look all sweaty, red, and out of breath?" I joked.

Melanie laughed and I joined her, encouraged by her comments.

"Have you ever been to Star Lake before?" said a deep voice from behind me. I spun around. *Clay!*

"No, this is my first time." *I hope I don't look like a*

moron.

"Cool. I hope you like it. Coach tells us to run here a lot."

"Hey, guys!" Tom yelled. "My house is close by. Turn there, and it's the third house on the right. Go down the driveway to the back fence. The hose is back there."

I stopped to tie my shoelaces, and all the guys left in a hurry so they could be the first ones in line, except Clay. When I looked up, he was standing there.

"Hey...I just thought I'd wait for you," he said. *Oh, my gosh! Did my heart just skip a beat?*

"Thanks," I replied. I stood up, and we headed for Tom's house. When we got there, the line was pretty short. Dawn was at the end.

"Finally! I get to cool off!" Dawn said with satisfaction as she waited. Jon was next in line. He took a long gulp from the end of the hose. Water dribbled down his chin and onto his shirt. Then, he bent over and ran water all over his head. When he finished, everything but his shoes was wet, and he handed the hose to Dawn. Dawn turned around to face Clay, who was next to her, and squirted the water all over her upper body drenching her white tee shirt. Still spraying herself, she poked her chest out as far as she could. She looked up at Clay and flashed her best smile.

The look on Clay's face was priceless. It was a look of pure disgust. "Gee whiz," he muttered to me with the "She's a moron!" look on his face.

"Give me the hose, Dawn." Clay said curtly.

"You've taken long enough." Dawn looked a little confused as she walked off, her shoes squeaking slightly from being wet. As Clay cooled off, I stared at him, my eyes following his every move. *He's so incredibly cute.*

"Jade! Earth to Jade! Are you okay?" Clay said, waving the hose in my face.

"Huh? Oh. Sorry, Clay. All this heat must really be getting to my head." I blushed a little as I took the hose from him. He watched me for a second and then jogged off. As soon as I was done, I handed the hose to one last teammate behind me and walked over to the picnic tables beside the lake. All I could think about was Clay, Clay, Clay.

Coach Bresler's voice hammered into my head, jostling my thoughts. "Boys! Get ready for intervals! Girls! Head back to school." The sun beat down again. *At least I had a tiny break from the heat.* I slowly started jogging back to the school. A few minutes later, I started to dry, and then I started to sweat again. The relief the water had given me was completely gone. The sun was zapping all of the energy out of me. By the time I climbed the gigantic hill to Berry, I was exhausted. I walked into the school and headed straight for the locker room. I stepped into a shower stall, turned on the cold water, and let it flow over my sweat-soaked head. *Man, this feels good. When I get home I'm gonna take a real shower.* It didn't matter how wet my shirt would get. It was already drenched in sweat. I turned off the water, flipped my hair back, and pulled a rubber band around it so it wasn't in my face.

As I moved through the halls, Mrs. Dillon passed me. "My! Aren't we looking lady-like today, Miss Montoya!" she said with sarcasm.

"Huh? Oh, the hair! It was really hot, Mrs. Dillon."

"Not just the hair, Dear. Your shirt is filthy, your legs are a strange shade of red, and you look as though you just woke up. Jade, we expect our students to look decent and respectable." Right then, Melanie walked up looking just as bad as I did. Maybe, even worse. "Well, Melanie! I hope you don't expect to look like that during the Beauty Walk."

"Don't worry, Mrs. Dillon. I only look like this after running four or five miles," Melanie apologized.

"Well, I saw Dawn a few minutes ago, and she looked fine," the staid teacher commented with a scowl on her face.

"Then Dawn must not have been running very hard and probably didn't get as much out of the workout as me and..." Melanie paused. "...I mean, Jade and I. We have to go now, or our moms will start to worry." She grabbed my wrist as we headed off toward the lockers.

Once we were out of Mrs. Dillon's hearing range, I exclaimed, "Thanks, Melanie! That was great! She yelled at me all of the time last year for taking the steps two at a time."

"She's a nut, huh?" Melanie said through giggles.

We packed our things from our lockers and started down the hall. I guess we had taken a while because we found Clay had already returned from practice and was at the end of the hall. Dawn was leaning against the wall next to him, rattling on about some problem of hers that he hopefully didn't even care about.

"Hey, Jade. Hey, Melanie," Clay said. "Y'all going home now?"

"Yeah. It's a long walk, so we better get going," Melanie replied.

"Why don't you let me drive you? I don't mind at all," he said.

"That'd be great, Clay. Thanks," I said, beaming.

"What about me?" Dawn pleaded.

"Sorry, Dawn, but I heard Jeff say that he was going to take you home. I'm not about to get into trouble with him."

"Fine!" retorted Dawn, as she stormed off.

"Let me go get my bag, and I'll be ready," Clay yelled over his shoulder as he walked away.

"Gee, Jade. If I didn't know any better, I'd say you've got a crush on Clay," Melanie said with one eyebrow raised. "Do you?"

"Shhhhh! Don't say anything," I begged. "He might hear."

"I'll find another ride, so you can ride alone with Clay. You didn't answer my que-" Melanie cut her sentence short because Clay walked up.

"Ready?" Clay asked.

"You two go ahead. I'll catch a ride next time," Melanie responded.

As Clay and I walked to his car, Dawn and her

friends marched up to us. Dawn jeered loudly, "Clay, I don't know why you're hanging around with a freak like Jade. You better stay away from her. She's bad news. ALL freaks are. She's trying to be a jock, but...oh, never mind." She paused with a smirk on her face. "Clay, why don't you come with my friends and me? We're going to Davenport's Pizza for cokes. We're meeting some others there."

"Don't worry, Jade. Dawn's just kidding," Clay reassured me. "Why don't you come too?"

Clay looked so sincere, like he really wanted me to come. I opened my mouth to say yes but noticed Dawn giving me the evil eye over Clay's shoulder. Her blue eyes hardened to a glossy ice, and her jaw tightened. *Do I really wanna risk getting her wrath?*

"That's really nice of you to ask, but I really have to be getting home," I lied.

"Oh," he said, disappointment filling his face. "Dawn, is Jeff gonna be there?"

"Yeah. He's getting his stuff right now," Dawn replied.

"Great. I'll take Jade home and then meet y'all there," Clay added.

"No. That's okay, Clay. You go ahead," I said. "I'll catch another ride. It's no big deal."

"Are you sure, Jade?"

"Yeah, I'm sure."

"Well, okay then," said Clay. He walked off toward his car. As Clay was about to hop in, he looked back and gave me an apologetic smile. The rest of them jumped into their cars and drove away. I turned and started the long walk home, feeling very dejected. *It had been a great day until Dawn showed up! Maybe Fern's right. Maybe all jocks are snobs. No, that's not right. Melanie's nice. But still...is it going to be like this everyday? Am I going to have to put up with being treated like that everyday? Is cross-country really worth that kind of rejection? I worked so hard to get Mom to let me run, but now it doesn't seem worth it. Nobody believes in me. Mom and Mrs. Dillon don't think it's lady-like, Dad's not here, Dawn's out to get me, Clay's...well...who knows...and the rest of my teammates...well most of them, anyway...probably don't even know I exist. I can't blame them for anything. Maybe I should just quit. That'd make everything so much easier.*

I had reached the convenience store at the bottom of the hill. Supper would be soon, so I decided to just get a drink. I grabbed a six-and-a-half ounce bottle of Coke. After I paid for it, I wearily started back home. *Coke is good, but I'll bet it's better at Davenport's with Clay.*

"DON'T...EVER...QUIT." Coach Bresler's words came back to me. *"There will come a time when you feel like you can't go on, but DON'T...EVER...QUIT. If you're too tired to run, walk. If you're too tired to walk, crawl. But quit? NEVER!"* I knew what I had to do. *Jade, you can't give up because of one obstacle, especially a social obstacle. You can't let someone like Dawn stand in your way. Stick with cross-country no matter what. It'll be great when Dad comes home. He'll be so proud of you.* "Thanks, Coach," I whispered to myself.

Dusty lay on the front porch waiting for me. He jumped up when I rounded the corner. "Hey, Dusty!" I said as my golden friend ran up to me. "I sure hope your day was better than mine."

I wearily swung open the front door, and Dusty followed me in. Mom jumped up from the living room couch. Excitement and happiness filled her face.

"Jade, some very important mail just came."

"What about?" I asked. A million things ran through my head. *Maybe it's the tax refund! Now I can get the Allman Brothers albums I've wanted for so long!*

"Your Dad's coming home!" Mom squealed.

"Ahhhhhhhh!" I screamed as Mom grasped me in a huge bear hug. "When? Tell me when!"

"I'm not sure. A month, maybe two, three... but it'll be soon," Mom said, a little less ecstatic. "Why don't we go to Lloyd's to celebrate!" she added cheerfully.

"Sure. I'll go get ready. I'm kind of nasty right now."

"Okay. I need to do some laundry anyway. Try and be ready in about forty-five minutes. Okay, Jade?"

"Great," I yelled over my shoulder as I walked into my room. I grabbed a towel and crossed the hall to the bathroom. Practice had made me anxious to take a long, hot shower. *This feels great, but Dad's coming home, and that's even better. I hope he's back in time for at least one of my meets.* When I stepped out, the mirror was fogged up and steam filled the bathroom. I jumped across the hall and slipped on a pair of jeans that I knew Mom would like. They were the bell-bottomed kind and weren't baggy at all. I had them left over from my "olden" days. I found an old red sweater that was a little short but fit okay. I stood next to the mirror and observed myself. *Whoa, I look like part of Dawn's "snob patrol." Oh, well, it's only for one night.* I walked over to my dresser to pick out socks and noticed a shiny red ribbon lying in the drawer. *I guess I'll go all out tonight.* I pulled my hair up and tied the ribbon around the ponytail. I put on my socks and a pair of sneakers.

"Mom, I'm ready!" I yelled down the hall.

"Okay, Honey. Let's go!"

I stepped into the living room, and Mom was standing there looking bewildered.

"What happened to the other clothes, Jade?" she inquired.

"It's just for tonight, so don't push it," I said, trying to get off the subject.

"Well, you look very nice. Would you like to drive tonight?" Mom asked.

My mother wants to know if I want to drive? Is this my mother speaking? She's probably wondering who I am and what I did with Jade, too.

"Sure," I replied as she threw me the car keys. We headed out the door with Dusty after us. Mom slid in her side. I opened my door, and as usual let Dusty in the middle.

"No way, Jade. Dusty goes in the back."

"Oh, okay. Come on, Boy, it's the back for you," I

said, opening the back door. Dusty hopped in grate-
fully. I rolled down his window, shut the door, and
slumped into my seat. I started the old Buick and
pulled out of the driveway. I could see Dusty in my
rear view mirror. He loved sticking his head out when
we drove. His ears flopped out behind him, and his
tongue lolled out. *Goofy dog.*

"I can't wait 'til Dad comes home." I paused. "I
know he'll be at all my meets... if he's back in time.
He always talked about how much he loved to run."

"Dad's not the only one who's going to be at your
meets," Mom said cautiously.

"I thought running wasn't lady-like, Mom."

"Well...things are changing. I can't make you be a
cheerleader. You'd never be happy. If cross-country
is what you love to do, then do it. I'm proud of you
for sticking with what you love and not doing something just because I wanted you to."

"Thanks, Mom." The rest of the way to Lloyd's
Restaurant I really bonded with Mom which was
weird. In that half-hour we connected the same way
we did that morning in the kitchen. We pulled into
the parking lot of Lloyd's. I made sure that I partially
rolled up the window so Dusty couldn't get away
while we ate.

Just before I left, I whispered in Dusty's ear,
"Don't worry, Buddy. I'll bring you back something."
Mom's heels clicked on the wooden floor as we
walked into the restaurant. After a waitress seated us,
we began to talk again.

"So, how was cross-country today?" Mom asked,

actually sounding interested.

"Oh, Mom! You'll never believe what happened today!"

NINE

SITTING AT THE DESK IN MY ROOM, I finished my homework and placed the pile of old, ragged textbooks next to my unmade bed to get them out of the way. As I was putting the pen and pencil back into their plastic cup next to the clock radio, I thought about my options for the dwindling evening. *I don't know whether I should watch* Adam-12 *on television or go to bed early and let my body recover from our killer practice. Maybe I should write Dad.* After much debate, I realized the significance of an unexpected letter as I remembered the joy I felt when I received one from him. *Maybe Dad will receive the same kind of blessing.* I was tired but determined to write even if it never got mailed. I refrained from putting the pen away and began.

Dear Dad,

How are you? I'm fine. I'm doing pretty well in school. Mom is fine, and so is Dusty. You'll never believe it, but I've decided to run cross-country. It's a one-mile race up and down hills. This is the first year Berry High School has formed a girls' team. The boys' teams have done really well the last few years, winning several state championships. The girls would like to continue this tradition by winning our first ever state meet. Mom didn't like the idea of me running at first, but I guess it kind of grew on her. Coach Bresler is wonderful. I'm proud to be part of his team. He works us pretty hard and has so much faith in us. Miss O'Neal is the one who encouraged me to run. She has no experience in coaching, so she's learning along with the rest of us.

Our practices take us on special courses that keep us away from the track. I love the "Hackberry Loop" because we start and finish downhill. We call it this because we have a solid mile of uphill to run on Hackberry Lane. It sure is hard, but it will make us better. The neighborhood next to the school is where our cross-country course is. I don't like running there because it seems as if we keep going uphill all of the time. I know that it goes downhill some, but it never seems like it. We run to Star Lake, too. Once we get there, it's pretty flat. Sometimes, Coach makes us run fast intervals around the lake. I don't mind going there too much, but the last hill coming back to the school is a killer after a long workout.

My least favorite route is the Sears Loop. I dread it because it is five long miles of busy and narrow streets. To start, we run a solid mile of uphill to Shades Mountain Baptist Church where we turn right and go to Canyon Road. Most of the time, we run in peoples' yards to avoid the on-coming traffic, but a few people have glared at us for doing that. Running on the grass is dangerous too because of chipmunk holes and unraked hickory nuts. If possible, I run through lawn sprinklers to cool off. It makes running this course a little better. When we get to Sears on Highway 31, we know we're halfway through. Once during this run, all the girls stayed together as a group, something we don't do very often. Everyone wanted to go inside Sears to get water and rest except me. They headed in, and I kept going all by myself. I really wanted to be part of the team but not by cheating. I couldn't believe that they actually did that. It was pretty hard to resist, but I was strong and continued on. My friend Melanie just looked at me in disbelief. I kept looking over my shoulder as I jogged slowly so they could catch up to me. I finally saw them coming a few minutes later down Highway 31, and soon they engulfed me in a cloud of anger and flying dust, speeding off at a fast pace. I struggled to keep up, determined not to be left behind. When we got to school, some of them wouldn't even talk to me in the locker room. They treated me as if I was invisible. I felt pretty lousy, and it really hurt my feelings, but I took it as best I could. At least everyone on the team didn't treat me like that.

    You're not going to believe what those crazy guys on the boys' team did. In their locker room, there is a huge commercial dryer with a window in the door. Joey, the equipment manager, got into the dryer with a football helmet on and toilet paper around his knuckles for padding. Clay, this guy on the team, pushed the button, and Joey started spinning. He was trying to beat his old record of eleven times around without getting sick. I saw the whole boys' team come out of the locker room door holding their stomachs from laughing so hard just before practice began. Then, just before the football coach went in, Joey wobbled out, half-heartedly smiling because he set the new record, twelve times around.

I guess my teammates paid me back for not stopping at Sears the other day. They told the coach about this big blister that was on my heel from the new pair of Pumas that Mom bought me. For the rest of my life, I'll never forget what happened next. Miss O'Neal called me into her room and asked, "Do you have a blister, Jade?" I knew I had made a mistake by saying, "Yes," when I turned and saw my so-called friends snickering and patting each other on the back as they crowded the door for a closer look. She cut the skin to let the water drain, then sprayed this "Nitro-Tan" stuff inside that hit the raw flesh underneath. Talk about pain! I started screaming and jumping all around while everyone else was laughing like crazy. I fought back the tears and thought how mean they were to do this to me.

I guess our coaches figured out that some of us (not me) were cutting the courses short. They gave us a run that couldn't be cut short. Coach Bresler drove us to the corner of Shades Crest Road and Highway 280 and dropped us off. "See you back at school," he said. It was a five-mile run with NO shortcuts. I was exhausted, but I was grateful that it wasn't as bad as the guys' practice. They had to run back to Berry from Eastwood Mall, which was over ten miles!

I stopped writing, racking my brain for forgotten

details. *Oh, Clay, would you ever do anything like cutting the courses? I don't THINK you would, but even the straightest arrows break!* I couldn't think of anything else to tell Dad, so I reread the letter. I discovered that writing these things down made me feel better, helping me to examine and explain my feelings. I finished...

I love you very much, and can't wait till your next letter. Please be careful. I hope you can come home soon. I'll keep you informed on my cross- country experiences. Gotta go.

Love,

Jade

I meticulously folded the letter and put it in an envelope to get it ready for mailing. The day's activities were finally catching up to me, so I knelt beside my bed and said my prayers. *I see the moon, and the moon sees me. God bless the moon, and God bless me...and Mom and Dad too, please. Thank you, God.*

*   *   *

"Today, I thought I'd let you run the trail," Coach Bresler said. "Y'all need a relaxed run for tomorrow's race. Don't over do it. Save it for tomorrow. It's not a race. Relax and have fun. Don't get hurt, and stay together as a team. Guys, you don't have to stay with the girls. Girls, don't try to keep up with the guys. Be back in thirty minutes, max!" *Great! I love to run the*

80

trails. The shading trees scrape the sunrays away.
That's one of the best parts of the trails...the shade. It
seems to be ten degrees cooler there. The scenery is
perfect in every aspect, like a painting. It takes my
mind off the running. The miles pass quickly.

We made our way through the front parking lot
and down to the tunnel. This tunnel was supposed to
be a safe haven when crossing the street, but it had
turned into a hangout. The very idea of that tunnel
both terrified and thrilled me. This was where students met for fights and where drugs were swapped
and used. Inside, the ground was littered with cigarette butts. The smell of mildew filled my nostrils,
gagging me with its intensity. I hurried the twenty
yards to get through it. The guys were gone, not
waiting for us. A relaxed pace for them was full speed
for us. When we ran the trails, we always stayed
together, so no one would get lost. We went different
routes each time unearthing hidden shortcuts.

"Jade, why don't you lead us today?" Dawn suggested.

"No, that's okay. I've never been this way before," I stuttered, surprised by the very idea.

"Oh, come on. You haven't led us before. It'll be
fun." She was prying me, so I accepted.

"Oh, all right." I said. *Wow, I can't believe they*
really want me to lead. That's an important responsi-
bility. Maybe they're all finally accepting me, a so-
called freak, as one of them. Maybe I've crossed the
barrier and all my hard work has finally paid off.

I soon found out that being the leader was not as

glorious as it seemed. I had to make decisions on which way to go, my teammates complained about the pace, and I constantly had to pull strands of spider webs off my face. We had run for about five minutes when we came to a fork in the trail.

"Which way?" I yelled.

Dawn yelled back, "Turn right!"

Relaxed, I turned and kept running. *This is fun, leading through the woods. I'm really glad that I decided to lead.* I ran about four more minutes when I came to another fork.

I yelled, "Now which way?" No answer. An uneasy feeling overcame me all of a sudden. Trying to avoid my fears, I refused to turn around. My pace slowed to a jog. *I haven't heard sticks cracking or anyone behind me breathing in a while.* I stopped, waiting for someone to bump into me, but no one did. I turned around, panicked to see nobody behind me as hurt and anger washed over me like a plummeting wave. *Maybe they're just further behind. Maybe I was going too fast. Yeah... that's it. I was going too fast. They'll be here in a few seconds. No need to worry.* But I wasn't convincing myself. I stood there, tears streaming down my cheeks. I was scared and angry and hurt all at once. I had never run this route before, and being alone in those woods was scary. I sat down and cried the tears that begged to be freed. *Come on Jade, this isn't going to do you any good. Crying never did anybody any good. Work through your difficulties.* My mind flashed back to the day I had skipped school and the lessons I had learned then. *You'll have to retrace your steps and find your way back. Come on, you can do it.*

After a few minutes, I regained control and stood up. I dusted the leaves that had accumulated on my sweat-dampened shorts and dried my eyes and red cheeks with the sleeve of my shirt. I slowly started walking, retracing my steps back to the tunnel.

"There you are, Jade," came a voice that surprised me. "I've been looking all over for you!" It was Melanie. I lost control.

"No you haven't! You helped set me up! All this time I thought you were my friend, but you weren't! You helped trick me! I've tried as hard as I could to make you like me, but NO...it was too much for a jock to like me. Y'all were angry because I didn't stop at Sears, so you paid me back by telling Coach about my blister. I can't believe that. I thought YOU would be different! I thought YOU would be nice!" I sagged to the ground and tried to calm down. "But, I guess I was wrong."

Melanie stared at me, disbelief written on her face. She sadly turned and walked slowly away. *What have I done? It wasn't supposed to happen this way. Melanie was supposed to apologize or at least SAY something. Now I'VE really messed up.* No longer concerned about being lost, I sat there and stared at the empty woods.

TEN

"BRIIIING!" THE PHONE RANG on my bedside table.

"Hello," I mumbled, trying to sound awake.

"Hey, Jade!" Fern said cheerfully. "I know it's late but you weren't home earlier. How was your day?"

"Hmmm..." I replied thoughtfully, trying to decide whether or not to tell Fern about practice. *She might be of some consolation. What could it hurt? Don't tell her about Dad though. She might ask too many questions.* "Dawn and her friends played a mean trick on me today at cross-country practice."

"You're kidding! What did they do?"

"I was leading the team while we were running. They left me stranded in the woods, and I was really scared. Melanie did come back to find me, but I blew up at her because she was as much at fault as the others. She didn't even say anything when I yelled at her. She turned and walked off, and I haven't seen or spoken to her since. Now I feel bad, like I should apologize to her."

Fern was silent on the other end of the phone. Then she said smugly, "I told you so. You don't need to tell her you're sorry. She's the one who should apologize. Jade, you don't know half the things Melanie does to my other friends and me. You think Dawn is mean, wait 'til I tell you about Melanie! She's egged my house twice, broken into my PE locker and stolen my clothes, and put them in the lost and found. And, she spreads rumors about me ALL the time."

"I can't believe that! Why?"

"Because that's how she treats freaks."

"But she's not like that to me, Fern," I protested.

"Yeah...well...that's because she knows you," Fern bitterly snapped. "She only THINKS she knows me." There was a short silence. "Well, I've got to go. See ya tomorrow."

"Bye." I stayed awake for what seemed like hours trying to digest everything that Fern had told me.

The next day after school, we were ready for our first meet. As the team headed to the bus, a few students, still at school for other activities, yelled, "Good luck!" *It feels good to be a part of something I'm proud of. Do the rest of the girls realize how big a breakthrough we're making? We are proving to everybody that girls are as important and capable as guys are. This first race will be a good time to show people what we're made of.*

I was in no hurry, unlike my other teammates, to pile into the bus. No one had even mentioned yesterday's prank. There was an uneasiness that I felt now with Melanie. *Should I bring it up or ignore it like we did on the bus this morning?*

I sat in an empty seat and pulled out my thermos of water and began to munch on some crackers. I was so nervous about my race that I had barely touched lunch. Trying to act cool, I turned and took a quick glance at the others on the bus. I was the only one sitting alone. *Was that Dawn sitting next to Clay? Great! Oh, well. At least I have plenty of room to myself, and I won't be crowded. That's the way to stay positive, Jade.*

Surprisingly, the bus was really quiet. *I wonder if everyone is as nervous as I am.* I stood to throw away my wrapper and felt as if everyone's eyes were on me. When I turned to sit down, I had a nice surprise waiting for me. Melanie was sitting in my seat.

"What are you doing here?" I questioned. She patted the seat next to her and coaxed me to sit down.

Without answering my question, Melanie replied, "So, are you ready?"

"Yeah, I think so," I said.

"What's wrong?" she asked.

"Nothing. I'm just really nervous."

"Yeah. Same here. So...Jade...I umm...I hope you're not mad at me."

"Well..."

Melanie continued, "I knew that they were gonna leave you in the woods and ditch you like that yesterday. But rather than spoil their fun, I kept my mouth shut. I should have warned you. I'm sorry. I should have told them not to do it, but I didn't. I could have, at least, run with you. I'm really, really sorry."

"Well, I WAS really scared. I still don't understand

why y'all did that to me. Was it your idea, Melanie?"

"No. It was Dawn's."

"What's she have against me? Do you know?"

Melanie squirmed in her seat and turned around to see if anyone was listening. When she knew she was safe, she replied, "Dawn doesn't like you. She calls you a freak. I've tried to tell her you're not like the rest of them...you're cool...but she doesn't believe me. I was afraid that if I didn't go along with her then she'd start hating me, too."

The bus turned the corner onto Gay Way as we headed to Vestavia High School. Everyone started laughing and making fun because of the name of the road. I hesitated to ask but decided to anyway, "Have you ever egged Fern's house before?"

Melanie erupted, "What are you talking about? Did she tell you that? You can't believe anything those freaks say. She was probably high and hallucinating when she told you that. You can't trust them, Jade. If I was you, I'd stay away from those freaks, like I've told you before."

"What has Fern ever done to you, anyway, Melanie?"

"What do you mean...what has she done? She doesn't have to do anything. She's a freak. That's bad enough."

"Is that why Dawn treats me the way she does...because she considers me a doped up freak?"

Catching Melanie off guard with my boldness, she stuttered, "Yes...no...I mean...you're different! I know you. When Dawn gets to know you..." The bus came to a sudden halt as we reached our destination, ending our conversation as Coach Bresler motioned for us to settle down so he could talk to us.

"Calm down and listen," he said. A few moments went by before the movement had ceased. "Okay...in a minute, we'll all get out and set up right over there." He pointed to some trees near an old fence. "Then, I want y'all to get a good warm-up. Yesterday at practice I went over what I want you to do. Remember that I want you to jog about a mile before your race. Do a few strides and stay loose until your race starts. Be ready and stretched so you don't get hurt. Y'all need to check out the course to see where you're going and plan your race strategy. Meet me near the starting line about five minutes before the girls' race begins."

The team began to move about once again. The mob of guys pushed and forced their way out of the bus. Then, the girls tensely stood up, and we made our way out. As I scooted past Coach, he blurted, "Hey, Jade... good luck today. Show them all what you're made of."

"Thanks, Coach," I mumbled. "I'll try my hardest." *I wonder if he heard about yesterday.*

As I stepped off the bus, I was immediately swept up in the rush of the other competitors. They were warming up and stretching, focused on getting ready to race.

Our team headed to the shaded area. Hurriedly, I walked with them and set my bag down next to the fence. I took one last swig of my water, placed the thermos in my bag, and began to get out of my orange and white sweat suit which was hiding my uniform beneath. I was almost ready to jog the course. I slipped on my running shoes and quickly laced them up.

Having taken longer than anyone else, I hurried to the starting line where I could see Melanie and the rest of the team. *Please don't leave me. We're supposed to warm up together.* We began to jog the course, and I was amazed at the neighborhood that we were running in. A towering house on the left had a steep roof that gave it the appearance of a castle. The lawns on the right side of the road overflowed with luscious green grass that looked as soft as a feather. Enormous trees scattered the yards where a couple of happy, young children were playing tag. *I wish we could live in a place like this. Maybe when Dad gets home.*

After we had made our way up the hill to the turning point, we coasted back down the way we had come and were soon back at the finish line. I sat down near the starting line so I could spend the next couple of minutes stretching near my competition. One of the girls from Vestavia spoke up, "Hey, there. My name's Elaine. How about you?"

"My name's Jade."

"Well, Jade...did you check out that course? It seems longer than a mile, doesn't it? At least we have that big downhill at the end, though. I'm not sure I could make it without that downhill to the finish. Do you?" She smiled and acted very friendly, something I hadn't experienced in a while.

"Yeah, it seemed a little long," I responded. *She doesn't seem to think I'm weird. If she saw me in my apparently "freakish" clothes, would she still be this friendly? I wonder.* I enjoyed those few moments of equality.

Mom hurried to the group of parents that was assembled near the start/finish line. She waved and gave me a thumbs-up, and I waved back. To my surprise, the announcer declared, "Five minutes until we begin the girls' run. Five minutes." I thought my stomach would turn inside out. The butterflies were swarming, but they felt like bees.

Coach Bresler and Miss O'Neal ran up and began explaining, "Okay girls. The course is not too challenging...you've practiced on tougher than this. Don't go out too fast, and give us your best effort. You're making history today. Let's start our season out right. We'll be yelling for you, and we'll see you at the finish line."

"Good luck, Jade," Melanie piped.

"You, too," I said to Melanie, as Dawn joined her. "Good luck to you, Dawn."

She turned her head to me and snorted, "Hmph." She then turned back and walked away while mumbling, "You're the one that needs the luck."

WILL THIS NEVER END? Oh, well...you've got a race to concentrate on now.

I found myself tensed as the announcer explained, "I'll give you a two-count command. On your marks, and then the gun will go off. Good luck to all you ladies. Here we go."

When the gun went off, I sprinted up the hill and, before I knew it, the race was over. Mom was there to hold me up as I beckoned for a drink. She told me over and over how proud she was of me. When I came to my senses, I was proud of myself, too. I didn't come in first, but I didn't come in last, either. I had given my best effort, and according to Coach Bresler, that made me a winner.

The guys were getting ready to run their race, so I walked over to wish Clay good luck. As I approached him, he gave me a high five and exclaimed, "Oh...hey, Jade! Great race!" I beamed and wished him luck in return. As I walked over to be with the rest of my team, Mom, Coach Bresler, and Miss O'Neal all stopped me before I made it there to congratulate me on a hard run. It was thrilling to have so many people patting me on the back and telling me how well I had done. I felt like I was as light as a feather. When I made it to my bag, Dawn and two other girls from my team were standing there comparing their races.

"Hey! Great job y'all!" I greeted them excitedly. "We made it through our first one!" They looked at me quizzically with smirks across their faces and didn't respond right away. *Is a simple word of encouragement too much to ask from them?*

Finally, Dawn jeered, "NICE TRY TODAY! Better luck next time!"

ELEVEN

AFTER DAWN'S COMMENT at our first meet, I became determined to outrun her, something I didn't do in that first meet. I spent the next month running each practice and race as if it were my last. Still, Dawn always finished slightly ahead of me. Finally, I had another chance to beat her.

The buzzing energy preceding that day's meet seemed out of place for such a tranquil setting at such an early hour. Footprints marred the frosty dew that had settled on the grass the previous night. A flock of crows, squawking with anger at their forced premature awakening, populated one of many oak trees fingering the lavender sky. People wandered busily, aimlessly, like ants. My nervously churning stomach starkly contrasted the scene.

"Thirty minutes," crackled the announcer's loud-speaker. My muscles, tense from anticipation, needed badly to be stretched. I walked toward my team's mat, scanning its inhabitants. *Melanie isn't here*, I noted, and I quickly turned to the left. I didn't want to use my energy dealing with Dawn and her friends' antago-nism.

I found a tree protruding from the brim of the wood. Planting my hand on the trunk, I began to stretch. Visualizing the tension, nervousness, and energy melting from my body, I utilized breathing and mantra techniques I learned from an article on yoga and meditation that Fern had given me. Then, refreshed and limber, I trudged back to my coach and team for a last-minute pep talk.

"Miss O'Neal isn't here today," said Coach Bressler in his gruff voice. "You're on your own. I don't wanna make you nervous," — I flinched, knowing he didn't worry about such pettiness with the guys—"so just run hard, race tough, and gut it out." Melanie still had not arrived.

I felt my esophagus twist into a knot, then a lump rose up into my throat and clogged my breathing. The toast that seemed harmless at breakfast had undergone mitosis, reproducing itself repeatedly so that a heap of semi-digested mush now sat ready to lurch out of my mouth. As the starter cocked the gun, my legs instinctively fumbled into their place on the line and then turned to lead. The buzz of voices previously circling my head were suddenly hushed, and-

"POW," banged the starting gun. The mass collection of energy combusted as bodies fought and flailed for position. Elbows jabbed my sides as I dodged a seemingly infinite collection of frenzied spiked shoes, and I concentrated on converting my nervous energy into forward motion. It was strange running without Melanie to pace me, but I quickly adapted, growing to find the freedom refreshing.

Stay calm. Just a few minutes more, then it's all over. Soon my strides began to lengthen, my muscles loosen. *I could run like this forever.* I relished the sense of release. After about half a mile, a pang of nausea stabbed my abdomen. My lungs were starving. My throat burned, the tube of hot flesh not prepared for the icy oxygen being drawn into it. My legs grew heavy, and my knees tried to lock. *I wish I could transcend from my body, if only for one second, just so I don't have to feel this. Detach from the pain, Jade. Only four hundred yards to go.*

I compared the race to an army marching into battle, hungry for pain and deriving a high from such extreme measures of discipline. An image of Vietnam soldiers creeping stealthily from swamp to jungle to swamp in perpetual agony materialized in my mind. I pushed it out, my stomach too volatile for gruesome thoughts of war.

As I entered the straightaway, the crowd's roar hit me like a sonic boom. I blocked out reality and focused only on moving my legs with a more concentrated determination than ever before. The world flew past me with a whirlwind blur. I saw the finish line flash under my feet, then dropped to my knees. A parent forced me up and shoved a card that showed my finishing place into my hand, then pushed me, defenseless, into the sweaty mass of humanity.

For one delirious moment, I was not sure what I had just done, where I was, or what I was supposed to do next. When I came to my senses, I was on the fringes of the crowd, crouched over a mound of runny vomit, mouth bitter with the hard taste of bile. Physical discomfort was temporarily forgotten as I realized I had just run my best race of the season. I was the fourteenth finisher, fast enough to receive my first-ever award. I had also finished ahead of Dawn by two places. For the first time, she didn't take home a medal. The thin smile that spread across my face didn't seem to fit such a haggard body as I envisioned myself being called to accept my coveted trophy and basking in a symphony of applause all the way to and from the man presenting them.

"Great job!" exclaimed Miss O'Neal, knocking me down from my imagination and back onto Earth. "That's better than you've done all year!" She flinched ever-so-slightly at the sight and smell of my former gastric contents. "Sorry I'm so late," she continued. "I got caught in traffic. There was an accident. There were a couple of ambulances, and I think I heard someone say that one kid from Berry got hurt pretty badly, possibly killed."

With a knotting of my stomach, I realized "one kid" might have meant Melanie. *Yesterday, she was so excited, chattering incessantly about the meet. Nothing short of a crisis could make her skip.* "Th-that's terrible," I stammered, waving her off with a limp, shaky arm. *Melanie is the closest person I have to a friend on the team. What would I do without her?* I shuddered, not wanting to think of the possibility.

I made my exodus before the awards ceremony began to embark on a long, silent ride home. Mom's efforts in conversation were futile as my subconscious wandered defiantly always settling on Melanie. *What would happen if she died? Without anyone to talk to, would I admit defeat and quit the team? No...she would want me to keep at it. How much pain was she in? What if she's paralyzed? As passionate as Melanie is about sports, that could...*

Pulling into the driveway, my seatbelt was off and the door thrust open even before Mom turned off the ignition. I could feel the release of adrenaline as I raced, heart pounding as forcefully as a bass guitar in a metal band, to Melanie's trailer. I cleared the steps to her wooden front porch in one leap. With a trembling hand, I knocked on the front door. No answer. I knocked again, more strongly, and this time a middle-aged woman with a solemn face appeared in the doorway. She said nothing. The blood drained from my face.

"Oh, no!" I gasped. I could feel my lips move, but it didn't seem like me talking. It was as if my consciousness had evaporated, and I was operating solely on instinct. I bit my tongue and clenched my jaw, not sure whether I was fighting the urge to cry or scream. "Oh, no," I echoed. "Is Melanie alright?"

TWELVE

"UM...YEAH, MELANIE'S ALRIGHT." The woman looked confused. "Please, come in."

Melanie was sitting on the couch. Her skin was red and flushed. Tears glossed her face and spilled into her hair, making it limp and stringy. Her eyes were bloodshot and rimmed by a smoky smear of mascara. "Hi, Jade," she managed between sobs.

Relief gushed through my bloodstream. "Oh, Melanie, you're okay. But, what happened? Why are you crying?"

She burrowed her head into her hands, massaged her eyelids, and looked back up. "It's Tripp," she whispered, her voice hoarse and barely audible. "He's the one. The dead one. From the accident. Did you hear?"

"Yeah, I heard someone may have been killed, but I thought it might have been you," I said dumbfounded. I paused for a moment to let the information sink in. "Tripp? Dead? I can't believe it." I furrowed my brows, trying to understand why she was so upset. I knew Tripp pretty well; we'd hung out in the smoking pit and stuff. But as far as I knew, Melanie had never even spoken to him.

"Why'd you think it was me?" she questioned.

"You didn't show up at the meet, and..." I didn't feel like explaining any further. "Are you okay, Melanie?"

She drew a struggled breath and continued. "Yesterday, he asked me for help in math. You know, he was a freak. He had long hair and seemed to always smell like cigarettes, and he likes that weird music." I detected a hint of cringe in her face as she spoke. "Anyway, when he asked me, I didn't know what to do. I was with Dawn and a few other girls, so I just started making fun of him." She cringed again, this time with contempt for herself.

"I told him that maybe if he'd stop killing all his brain cells, if he stopped smoking so much pot and dropping so much acid, that he might have enough cells left to do his homework." Her voice was tainted by efforts at stifling sobs. "I called him a pot-head and a devil-worshiper, and I said that I bet his parents were druggies, too if they hadn't overdosed already." Melanie's tears started welling up again. I swallowed hard, and she continued, "Those were the last words I ever spoke to Tripp. I've never seen someone look as hurt as he did right then, and I thought it was funny. Now it's too late to..." Melanie struggled to continue, then added, "What am I going to do?"

I winced with restrained anger as I tried to imagine how Melanie could have been that cruel. Tripp was my friend. Still, my heart ached at the sight of her this visibly guilt-ridden. "It could've happened to anyone, Melanie," I assured her. "You don't have to torture yourself like this."

She was oblivious to my attempts at consolation. Having run out of tears, she was now rocking back and forth with a glazed distance to her eyes, mumbling to no one in particular. "And it was all because he dared to talk to me," she moaned.

THIRTEEN

MY THOUGHTS BUZZED as I walked toward the school's gymnasium that Monday morning. The death of Tripp had given me a newfound sense of the importance of life. I knew something needed to be done...something amazing...to make up for the loss of him...but...what? *I wish I could end our calloused way of life and open new doors...doors that shout harmony, peace, and love.*

As I entered the gloomy atmosphere of our gym, I realized that I had never been to a memorial service before. I had never even known anyone who had died before. *It's a weird feeling, knowing he's gone. I'll never be able to say "Hey" to him again, never see him walking down the halls, laughing and joking with friends, or look up from my desk to find him sitting in front of me in class. Now that Tripp is gone, it feels like there's an empty spot in my heart...a spot that maybe no one can fill but him.*

Standing in the front of the gym looking back, my eyes fell upon the whole student body. Some had somber faces while others were still cutting up and stifling laughs among quiet whispers that echoed throughout the room. To tell you the truth, that kind of made me mad. I mean, only a few of these students even wanted to be there. They didn't really care about Tripp. They only came because everybody in the school had to. I was looking for Melanie but could not find her in the bleachers or amidst the rows of folding chairs that had been set up for this special occasion. So, not wanting to be too close for comfort or too far away to see and hear, I sat down in a chair halfway up the aisle. Just when it looked as if Melanie had decided to skip school, she slipped through the crowd and found an empty seat next to me. I saw in her eyes the courage it must have taken for her to even be there. I tried to analyze what she must have been thinking right then, but all I could see was a tired face with sad red eyes. I knew that nothing I could say would make her situation better, so I took her hand in mine and held it tightly, hoping this action would say it all.

The students began to hush as our principal, Mr. Green, wearing a weary smile on his face, walked up to the podium. His voice, penetrating through the speakers, was mellow-toned and didn't seem worthy to be telling the story of Tripp's life. After several weepy people had come and "said a few words" about how wonderful his life had been and how Tripp had moved on to a better place, I was getting a little aggravated. I mean, sure...the speeches were sweet and comforting, but there had to be something more to it than that...didn't there? What was really important had been left unsaid.

As I stopped staring into space, my eyes settled on Mr. Green who had begun the memorial. "Is there anyone who would like to say something before we close?" he asked. I knew that this was my only chance to say what I knew the world needed to hear, and if I didn't speak up, I would always look back in regret. "Anyone?" he echoed.

My stomach felt like it was about to jump out of my body. My heart raced wildly as never before. I didn't hear the rest of what was said, and before I realized what was going on, I was standing behind the podium. A tingling crawled up my spine as I noticed that all eyes were on me. My face burned, and I felt my hands become clammy. The air had a tense coolness as I hesitantly stepped up to the microphone, trying to keep my knees from locking and looking awkward at the same time.

"Hello," I stammered, making sure the mike worked. Just when I started to wonder why I was doing this, a wave of boldness overcame me as I spied Fern kneeling tall in the back row and giving me a knowing smile. Her smile gave me more confidence than ever, and I began to let my feelings flow.

"I have been sitting in the chairs appalled at what I've been seeing and hearing. Some of you sit here and grieve about how you miss Tripp and how much you want him back, but it seems to me that you didn't care too much when he was still alive. Now that he's gone, I guess you figure it's okay to say, 'Oh, I liked him so much!' Why didn't you say so when he was here, when he could appreciate it? I suppose that was too much for you because you might be made fun of for liking a freak. Well, you know what? It's too late now. Tripp is GONE!

"Those of you who have been rude, inattentive, and downright disrespectful need to listen up. Have you ever hurt someone...not physically...but really hurt someone only because that person didn't measure up to your 'standards of excellence?' It's amazing how we can pity ourselves in our times of affliction, but it is even more amazing how we can bear the sufferings of others. When I first moved here, I didn't know anyone. By making one split-second decision at where to sit at lunch, I was labeled a freak by many of you. Later, when I decided to turn-the-tables by joining cross-country, no one knew what to think. Since I was doing a sport, did that make me a jock or a freak? So, instead of making me feel welcomed...wanted...I was shunned, treated as a reject. Close friends turned against me and...for what? ...for pursuing the things I enjoy most in life? Is that so much to ask?

"Tripp was not a loser like many of you may think. You may have known about what he wore and maybe who his friends were, but how many of you even knew who he was before this accident? Did you know his name, or did you just call him, 'That Freak?'

"We all need to take a moment, and look deeper. Did you know that Tripp worked late at night so he could help his mom pay the bills from his brother's leukemia? Their life-savings are gone. Did you know that Tripp spent most Saturdays at the nursing home tending to his sickly grandmother? Did you know that he was first chair trumpet player, or does that not matter because it's not cool like football or cheerleading? Few of you gave him a chance because he had long hair and wore peace signs around his neck. If we have anything to give to this world, it's through expressions of our different personalities. Without them, this world wouldn't amount to much. Besides...we're not so different after all.

"Most great people in life have something that makes them stand out, something different. Tripp was a great person. Wait...did you even consider him a person? We all make life too difficult by separating and judging when life could be so much simpler if we would all love each other...treat each other like dignified human beings. Look...I know that around here...jocks are supposed to be mean to freaks, and freaks are supposed to be mean to jocks...but before I moved here I guess I was naïve enough to think that people could treat each other with respect.

"Most of you are so intent on judging others that I was even afraid to admit that my father is a soldier in Vietnam. I never even told my closest friends for fear of rejection and ridicule. Well, now it's out in the open. Yes, my father is in Vietnam. I don't think you realize the pain and torture those soldiers must endure...and their families, too. It's not fair to automatically judge them the way you do...as drug addicts and baby killers. They are real people—with the same feelings and needs as each of us. They need love and friendship just like each of us...just like jocks...just like freaks. A real friend doesn't judge.

"Real friends are those who look at the heart...inside it. Friends don't care about appearance but look in much deeper. They value your individuality...yours, as well as others. The things you say and do can make or break a person's day. A simple smile once rescued me from everything.

"We have been given a golden opportunity to right our wrongs. There is still time. There is a barrier between some of us that needs to be broken. Let us use the lessons we can learn from Tripp's death to break through that barrier.

"The death of Tripp Garner is truly a pain to all who knew him, but out of this pain we can find joy. Unexpected trials can make us into better people. Now, we have this chance to put aside our differences and stand up for what we all know is right. If we don't want his life to go to waste, we must act now. We all claim to have dreams of changing our world, and making it a better place, but don't we have to be willing to change ourselves first? The choices we undergo mold our lives, and our lives mold the world. Everyone has his or her own free will...no one can decide for you! Do you want to be a mindless con-formist, or do you want to change lives? I'm telling you, one spark can start a fire. Please, I challenge someone in this room to take the first step...just...try. Is there someone here today whom you've wronged...someone that you don't even know that you've stereotyped? Surely, if Tripp could, he would tell us that life is much too short to hold judgment against anyone. You must do the right thing while you can. I beg of you to act now. Go...now...and apologize...if that's what you need to do. Go...now...and let the healing begin."

I drew a deep breath, not believing the things that I had just said. I looked around at everyone sighing in disbelief. My fellow students had their heads bowed, staring blankly at the floor, desperately trying to avoid eye contact with anyone. A long, awkward silence filled the room as all the students held their breath, not a soul making a noise, waiting to see what would happen next. The crowd turned in unison upon hearing the high-pitched squeak of a chair moving across the wooden floor and saw Melanie slowly standing to her feet. All eyes were upon her as she shook silently, a flood of tears streaming from under the clutched hands that were covering her face. As she squeezed through the rows of chairs, everyone stared to see what she was going to do. I couldn't believe it. She was heading to the back of the gym.

The look on Fern's face was unmistakable as it filled with disbelief. The two looked at each other, wiping away tears, and although they didn't say a word, their faces told it all..."everything will be okay." As they fell into each other's arms, a miracle swept through the entire room. You could literally see all of the superficial boundaries dissolving. One by one, students rose like a chain reaction, speaking words of forgiveness and regret. People who had never talked before were laughing and crying and hugging each other. Before long, they were joking like old friends. I walked down from the podium feeling as light as air.

Joy this immeasurable had yet to exist in my life before. I knew that things wouldn't be perfect from now on, but I also knew that this school...this city...would never be quite the same.

As the students dispersed for their scheduled classes, a few remained behind. I made my way to the door and heard a familiar voice calling my name.

"Jade, over here!" I turned around and was delighted to see that it was Clay. He looked like he had been crying. I never thought that I would see tears on that heavenly face. He walked up closer to me and stared into my eyes. I felt like he could see straight into my thoughts.

"You don't know how much you mean to me, Jade. What you said was the most profound thing I've ever heard. I've never known a girl who could get up there and do something like that." He stepped closer, leaving only inches between us and wiped a tear from my cheek.

Just as I felt myself go weak at the knees, Clay's strong arms wrapped around mine. I felt as if nothing could ever go wrong as long as we were standing like this in each other's arms. Letting go, he gave me a peck on the cheek, flashed me one of those gorgeous smiles, and before I knew what was happening, he was out the door.

My heart melted into a puddle as I realized he had kissed me...Clay had really kissed me! I looked around the room so I could remember how everything looked. I wanted to remember this day...forever.

EPILOGUE

The overcast sky spills fat droplets of moisture as I walk home from school. I bow my head to keep the water out of my eyes, instead letting it penetrate my layer of hair to shock my scalp with a chill. My shoes are soggy from sloshing through puddles. The wetness of my clothes pushes cold deep beneath my skin until even the marrow of my bones feels frozen. I shudder and brace myself for warmth. It is early December 1974, and the gloomy atmosphere implied by the weather has me in a reflective mood. Dad has been home for a week now. It was weird when he first arrived here. For the year he was at war, I imagined him as a happy, carefree hero who would return and make my life perfect. He'd entertain me with war stories and songs that he and his soldiers had thought up to help dilute the agony of battle. It hasn't been like that at all. I always thought that when Mom and I met him at the airport, his lips would stretch into a smile, and he'd hug us, laughing. In reality, the only hint of emotion haunting his face was a little wetness that accumulated in his eye and drizzled down into his beard. And he's spent the past week incessantly sullen and withdrawn.

I slowly turn, then push the slippery doorknob and step inside, making sure to remove my water-logged shoes before continuing further. Still cold, I pull my coat from the rack and slip it on. Mom is in the kitchen, hovering over the stove. The smell of onions wafts the air.

I continue down the hall and into my room. Dad is sitting on my bed with a faraway look in his eyes, clutching the pieces of the pot that Melanie had broken months ago. If he notices me, he doesn't show it.

"Hi, Dad," I whisper awkwardly. "What's going on?"

He jumps, apparently startled. "Oh...hey, Jade. Remember when we made this?" He holds up the pieces.

"Yeah," I respond. "I was only eight years old." I close my eyes and sigh. "I wish things were still like they were back then...you know...simple."

He furrows his eyebrows, carving a wrinkle in his forehead. "Don't say that."

"Why not?"

"What's wrong with your life now?" he asks, adopting a serious tone.

I'm surprised at how difficult the question is to answer. I had thought I was miserable, but maybe not. "Um...well, there's the jock-freak conflict at my school," I say uneasily.

He exhales loudly. "That's other people's lives. Tell me something that has to do with YOURS."

My mind races, searching for a problem. Its

search ends fruitless. "Oh...uh...I don't know," I stammer, trying to buy myself time. Dad recognizes my tactics.

"See, you're not bad off," he says. "Sure, you've gone through some tough stuff in the past year or so. It's hard moving to a new school as a junior and even harder when your choices clash with those of your friends. It's hard to lose someone like you did with Tripp at his age. It's hard to stand up like you did at Tripp's memorial service and defy the very customs that define a group of people. But, you suck it up and get through the tough times. Then, the easy times are that much better."

Beginning to understand, I nod. "Yeah. When you were in Vietnam, I'm sure there were some times when you were ready to just give up. With war being such a horrible thing, plus all the controversy here at home, you had to undergo some pretty intense agony. But, you gutted it out...and after a year of crawling through swamps, watching your friends die one after another...and knowing you were being called some pretty harsh names...you got to come home. And all that misery makes home feel even warmer."

He smiles, one of those fatherly "I've done good" smiles. It's the first time in over a week that I've seen him express any emotion. "See, Kid, you're gonna be all right," he teases. "Life is just like a war or a cross-country meet; you get through the pain, and it's all good." We laugh at the absurd metaphor.

I realize that this is the first time since coming to Hoover that I haven't felt some degree of pity, and probably the first time since leaving for Vietnam that Dad hasn't had to drown his feelings with the detached indifference necessary for a successful battle. I blink back a sprinkling of tears as he chokes a sob. Then, he extends beyond his declared realm of personal space that has been present since Mom and I picked him up from the airport. His thickly muscled arms, encircled around me, are comforting, and I can smell his spicy after-shave. We both cry. Life is good.

Unraked Hickory Nuts